MY MOTHER, THE DETECTIVE

BOOKS BY JAMES YAFFE

THE "MOM" MYSTERIES

A Nice Murder for Mom
Mom Meets Her Maker
Mom Doth Murder Sleep
Mom Among the Liars
My Mother, The Detective: The Complete "Mom" Short Stories

FICTION

Poor Cousin Evelyn and Other Stories
The Good-for-Nothing
What's the Big Hurry?
Nothing but the Night
Mister Margolies
Nobody Does You Any Favors
The Voyage of the Franz Joseph
Saul and Morris, Worlds Apart

NON-FICTION

The American Jews
So Sue Me!

PLAYS

The Deadly Game
Ivory Tower (with Jerome Weidman)
Cliffhanger

My Mother, THE DETECTIVE

THE COMPLETE "MOM" SHORT STORIES

JAMES YAFFE

CRIPPEN AND LANDRU PUBLISHERS   NORFOLK, VIRGINIA   1997

The stories were originally published in *Ellery Queen's Mystery Magazine*: "Mom Knows Best," June 1952; "Mom Makes a Bet," January 1953; "Mom in the Spring," May 1954; "Mom Sheds a Tear," October 1954; "Mom Makes a Wish," June 1955; "Mom Sings an Aria," October 1966; "Mom and the Haunted Mink," March 1967; "Mom Remembers," January 1968.

ISBN (limited edition): 1-885941-10-2

ISBN (trade edition): 1-885941-11-0

FIRST EDITION

10 9 8 7 6 5 4 3 2 1

Printed in the United States of America on acid-free paper

Crippen & Landru, Publishers
P. O. Box 9315
Norfolk, VA 23505-9315
USA

Letter to Fred Dannay

Dear Fred,

This is the book you said you wanted somebody to publish some day. It owes its existence, of course, to the enthusiasm and dedication of the publisher, Douglas Greene, but first of all to your skill as an editor and your generosity as a friend.

That was over forty years ago. I was too young and foolish in those days to appreciate what you did for me. How I wish I could thank you now.

All my love,

Jim

CONTENTS

INTRODUCTION

I got hooked on detective stories when I was seven or eight years old. The first one I ever read, as I recall, was Conan Doyle's "The Red-Headed League," and I have loved detective stories ever since. Like many love affairs, however, it has been agitated by eruptions of disillusionment, neglect, and outright hatred.

My ideas about the detective story have gone through three phases:

First, as a kid, what mesmerized me was the puzzle, and the peculiar satisfaction that came when I found out its solution. I recognized early on that I wanted this solution to be a surprise, though what surprised me then, of course, wouldn't surprise me very much now. In my innocence almost any ploy, no matter how obvious or heavyhanded, could fool me.

That was a great state to be in, I realize now. It was Detective Story Eden, when the helpful self-effacing Best Friend didn't arouse even the smallest twinge of suspicion in me, when you could bowl me over with the amazing news that the butler did it. (Actually I have yet to read a detective story in which the butler did it.)

My age of innocence didn't last long. Pretty soon I was seeing through most of the standard tricks. I came to understand that, when the heroine is loved by two of the male characters, one of them must be the murderer; that a body burned or otherwise mutilated beyond recognition is sure proof that the apparent victim isn't really dead; that the character who is charged with the crime early in the story but is later cleared and released will turn out to be the guilty party after all; and, in detective movies, that the presence in the cast of a highly expensive actor who doesn't seem to have anything to do means that he will ultimately be revealed as the murderer.

As I grew older and more experienced, it became harder to fool me, and I became more scornful of those who failed. I lost interest in the Phantom, a pulp magazine serial hero of my childhood, because the final revelation of Mr. X's identity was always thunderingly obvious in the first chapter. I also lost interest in some much better known and more respectable detective heroes—S. S. Van Dine's Philo Vance, for instance, who was always helped along in his investigations by the murderer's thoughtful habit of killing off all the other suspects before the book was two-thirds through. And I became impatient with stories in which the detective simply announced at the end that So-and-so was guilty, without benefit of any clues or logical deductions. I am still impatient with such stories, and I find a lot of them nowadays.

And yet, even in my childhood phase, it wasn't only the puzzle in its essence that attracted me. I never much enjoyed the detective puzzle books that were published with some success in the 1930's and 1940's; on each page a different "case" was summarized, and the reader challenged to find the solution and then look it up in the back of the book. The trouble with these capsule puzzles was that they deprived me of the *experience* of the story—the discovery of the crime, the unearthing of clues, the questioning of witnesses, the second murder that forced me to revise my previous theories, and the slow inexorable buildup to the great final scene, all the suspects gathered around the table, the great detective slowly unwinding his web of reasoning, the moment of revelation postponed as long as possible. I can remember with perfect clarity the almost unbearable thrill of that moment, as the villain's name sprang out at me from the last paragraph of the penultimate chapter.

As a kid I used to hold my hand over that last paragraph (while I read the next to last paragraph) for fear that I might be tempted to glance quickly ahead and spoil the surprise for myself one minute sooner than necessary. Sometimes I find myself making that same gesture in detective books I read today.

Because I decided at a ridiculously early age that I wanted to be a writer (if I had only known then what I know now, etc.), it was inevitable that I should begin by trying to write the kind of story I had always loved so much. My maiden effort was made at the age of twelve or thirteen when I had a two-week bout with the measles. Every day, lying in bed, I produced a chapter of a detective novel. My sister, fourteen years older than I, read these chapters when she dropped in to visit me. All I remember of her reactions was that she laughed her head off as she read; this puzzled me because nothing I had written was meant to be funny.

A few years later, at the age of fifteen, I wrote my first detective short story and sent it in to *Ellery Queen's Mystery Magazine*. Its editor was Frederic Dannay, one half of the Ellery Queen collaboration. He was not only a great detective story writer but the best editor in the world and a genuine scholar and penetrating critic of the form. It didn't take any Ellery Queen, however, to detect the juvenility of the writer of that first story, and I assume that was why Fred Dannay decided to publish it. It became the first of half a dozen that I wrote in the next two years, all about a detective named Paul Dawn who headed a branch of the New York Police known as The Department of Impossible Crimes.

The absurdity of this concept is a dead giveaway to what was really happening. The detective story to me, in that stage of my life, was the puzzle and nothing but the puzzle. The excitement of un-raveling the puzzle, which had been aroused in me by so many writers during my childhood, was pretty much all I was trying to reproduce in my own work. It was a game, and I was having an awful lot of fun playing it.

And I didn't play it too badly either. I was pretty sloppy and in-accurate from time to time (for two of the stories Fred Dannay had to append an editor's note inviting the reader to figure out the big logical flaw that rendered them totally invalid); but I was also from time to time fiendishly ingenious. Sometimes I think I reached my peak of sheer cleverness at the age of seventeen in the last couple of Paul Dawn stories; it's been downhill ever since.

But the one thing those early stories never had was any con-nection with reality. My central character's totally artificial name was one symptom of this. Fictional detectives, it seemed to me, were sup-posed to have mannered, rather fancy-sounding names, like Ellery Queen, Gideon Fell, Reggie Fortune, Sherlock Holmes. It simply never occurred to me to base any of my characters on people I had known or observed, to draw on experiences I had actually had, to set the stories in a social world I had lived in. Detective stories obviously *had* no connection with reality; that was part of what made them fun.

MY MOTHER, THE DETECTIVE

My inspiration and model wasn't real life, but other detective stories.

✤ ✤ ✤

Then, at the age of eighteen, near the end of World War Two, I was drafted into the U. S. Navy, and Paul Dawn suffered an early and much deserved demise. I got out of the Navy and went back to college, and my attitude towards detective stories was one of hostility.

I had discovered "real" literature, and suddenly I was reading novels not because they took me away from reality but because they pulled me more deeply into it. They made me a part of all kinds of real worlds whose existence I had never suspected before, from the slums of Dickens' London to the drawingrooms of Edith Wharton's uppercrust New York to the lockerrooms of Ring Lardner's baseball players. Above all I was excited by the fundamental enterprise of all fiction writers, no matter how different from one another in other ways: the creation of characters.

I wanted to do what Dickens, Wharton, and Lardner had done, create complicated flesh-and-blood characters based on the kind of people I knew from the world I grew up in. This ambition, I'm afraid, made me rather ashamed of poor Paul Dawn and the stories I had published in my callow youth. And my shame carried over to detective stories in general.

"Plot" was a dirty word in the climate of literary modernism that dominated American colleges in those days. (It is still a dirty word in the post-modern climate of today.) Victorian novels and Shake-speare's plays had plots, of course, but they were slightly embarrassing blots on the qualities that *really* made those works great. Detective stories, which seemed to depend entirely on plot, were beyond the pale—a judgment that was reinforced by the great critical guru of my college years, Edmund Wilson, in his famous diatribe, "Who Cares Who Killed Roger Ackroyd?", which appeared in *The New Yorker* while I was in college.

So I started writing "real fiction" and published some of it in magazines, leading to my first book, *Poor Cousin Evelyn and Other Stories*. Yet I didn't stop writing detective fiction—or even, in guilty privacy, reading it. Two years after college, I wrote the first "Mom" story, which opens this collection. My reasons for violating the principles

INTRODUCTION

I now claimed to believe in were purely pragmatic. I needed the money.

Or at least that was what I told myself. That writing the "Mom" stories—which I continued to do at intervals for the next fifteen years—also gave me enjoyment was a paradox I didn't care to examine too closely in those days. I told myself there must still be something child-ish in my nature, and I hoped I would be able to outgrow it some day.

Thirty years later I can see clearly that my ideas about detective stories were, in fact, moving into the second phase. The puzzle was still important to me; from my high aesthetic perch I may have started looking down my nose at the genre, but I was also determined to respect it in its own terms: puzzles may have been beyond the pale, but they still had to have a logical and ingenious solution, the author still had to play fair with the reader. But something even more im-portant than the puzzle was now capturing my imagination.

That was the character of the detective. I was attracted to this element through my newfound interest in character creation. If the central action is the unraveling of a puzzle, the character of the un-raveler must clearly be central too. The investigation of a crime whose wellsprings are hidden, whose details are apparently inexpli-cable, requires a protagonist who is superior to the ordinary run of humankind. In short, the detective must be a kind of genius, and the essential point of the detective story must be the characterization of such geniuses, how their minds work, how they relate to others and to society.

In its crudest form, this means relishing their external eccen-tricities. They are entertaining characters to the extent that they are weirder and wilder, not merely smarter, than ordinary human beings. Many practitioners of the genre have left it at that: but the great fictional detectives also display *meaningful* eccentricity, the kind that reflects some deeper aspect of their nature. I found myself enjoying Poirot's mustaches far less than the spunkiness with which he stands up to the stuffy English who look down on him because he is different from them. I found myself caring less about Sherlock Holmes' violin-playing and outlandish headgear than about his incurable melan-choly, the price genius pays for being forced to live in a world of dolts.

MY MOTHER, THE DETECTIVE

My new interest in fictional detectives—not simply as puzzle-solvers but as human beings who express their individual quirks and conflicts and inner demons through the *ways* in which they solve problems—led me to create Mom and write the stories about her that you will find in this collection.

People have asked me if I based her on my own mother. Nothing could be further from the truth. My mother was alive when the stories first appeared, and people asked her the same question, to her infinite embarrassment. Mom was not based on any particular person: I have given her different traits borrowed from different people I've known.

I have also given her many of the traits belonging to the familiar Jewish Mother stereotype: the pride in her children, the obsession with food, the kind of language she uses. These traits may be stereotypical, but they are also real; they can be found all the time in women of a certain generation and social group. My conviction is that we are all stereotypical in some ways, and it would be unrealistic for an author to leave that out in struggling to create a character. The point is to show the mingling within people of stereotypical and individual traits, to show the tug of war that goes on between what we are at heart and what the world tells us we should be—with neither side ever completely winning out.

So I tried from the start to give Mom a feistiness, a sharpness, an edge of cynicism as an antidote to the Warm Jewish Mother that she undoubtedly feels the need to be from time to time. I tried to show the streak of sentimentality in her, and then the sarcastic humor with which she mocks her own sentimentality. I tried to make her stand for certain admirable human values—she feels compassion for suffering and weakness, refuses to be taken in by phoniness, hates people who kill people—and at the same time I tried to show that sometimes she's a pain in the neck.

It has been pointed out to me that, in the course of these stories, Mom changes, seems to lose some of her snappishness. Reading the stories all at once, in chronological order, I recognize there is some truth to this. It was not done consciously; no pressure was ever put on me, by Fred Dannay or by complaining readers, to soften Mom up.

The reason she becomes a bit less abrasive, I think, is that I found myself probing her character more deeply with each story. At first I was simply amused by the incongruity of this simple Jewish mother beating the Homicide Squad at its own game, and the early stories operate on the level of exuberant farce. But eventually I began to delve into Mom's motivations, what her interest in her son's murder cases might reveal about her sufferings, joys, and contradictions as a human being.

I also began to understand how much the detective story can gain from attention to settings, backgrounds, specific cultures and societies. Sherlock Holmes' London is as sharply delineated as Dickens' London, and for the same reason: characters don't exist in the abstract, they don't float in space, they achieve life only by being solidly grounded in a particular social world. Mom's social world was always a part of the stories, but I think it gained solidity as I went along; it became less of a backdrop and more integral to the action of each story. By the time I got to the final story, "Mom Remembers," her social world was inseparable from the murder plot itself.

So now, at last, I had at the heart of my detective fiction a central character who was individual, believable, funny, and in her own way a genuine investigative genius. And yet, this was the point at which I abandoned Mom, abandoned the detective story, not to return to either of them for twenty years.

Hindsight tells me that I was on the verge of a breakthrough to the third stage—the final one, I think—in the development of my ideas about the detective story. But that breakthrough didn't happen; apparently I wasn't ready for it yet.

All through those fifteen years that I was writing the Mom stories, I was also writing realistic non-detective novels that dealt primarily with Jewish life in New York; at the same time I wrote three plays and two non-fiction books involving considerable research, and earned my living turning out scripts for television. Then I went off to Colorado College in Colorado Springs as a professor of literature and decided to concentrate, in my non-teaching periods, on "real" novels. For twenty years Mom disappeared into the same limbo as Paul

MY MOTHER, THE DETECTIVE

Dawn and the Department of Impossible Crimes.

What drew me back to the detective story about eight years ago was my discovery of the novels of the late Ross Macdonald. Actually I had read him earlier, but it was only now that I saw what he was really doing.

Macdonald's novels have every quality that appealed to me in the first two phases of my thinking about the detective story. They are highly accomplished puzzles, intricately and logically worked out. His detective, Lew Archer, is one of the most interesting and moving characters in post-war American literature: a human being with his own weaknesses and strengths, and a highly individual vision of life which makes him a troubled man but also allows him to succeed as a detective.

And the social and geographical settings of Macdonald's novels are created with far greater depth, it seems to me, than his own acknowledged masters—Hammett and Chandler—could ever quite achieve. Hammett's and Chandler's California, though unquestionably vivid, also strikes me as a bit picturesque, like stage sets (or maybe it would be more accurate to say movie sets). Macdonald's California and, in some of his books, Canada are real places; we *live* in them while the story goes on, they weigh on the heart.

In Macdonald's work the puzzle is no longer a blot on the novel's serious meaning but an integral part of it. The case that Archer takes on, the mystery-question that confronts him in the opening chapter, always has implications that go beyond Whodunnit. The investigation—that is, the central action—is designed to reveal different aspects of these implications to us. The "clues," the character of each suspect, the red herrings and violent interludes along the way invariably relate to the novel's underlying theme and take us more deeply into it. And the climax of the story—when we finally find out Whodunnit, and how and why—serves as the deepest revelation about that underlying theme. In *The Chill*, for example—one of his best—a stunning surprise at the end not only clears up the surface puzzle for us but also takes us into the heart of the deeper puzzle that revolves (as many of Macdonald's novels do) around the strange love/hate relationships between parents and children.

INTRODUCTION

In the four "Mom" novels that I wrote between 1988 and 1993 I tried to do something like this. I brought Mom and her policeman son to a thinly disguised version of Colorado Springs because I became interested in exploring the interaction between the denizens of Middle America and people who are outside the American mainstream. Mom, the inveterate New Yorker, but also an immigrant even in New York, seemed to be an ideal vehicle for this exploration.

The clash of different cultures is portrayed in each novel through a different setting that characterizes some aspect of smalltown Middle American life—a small college, an evangelical church, an amateur theatre, a politician's backroom. The murder in each novel is intended to cast significant light on the world of that setting. Mom's solution to the murder is achieved because of her ability to empathize with that world; at the same time, because she is a stranger with her own peculiar angle of vision, she can see what the inhabitants of that world can't see about themselves.

But all this sounds pretty heavy. I must add that, unlike Ross Macdonald, I see the detective story as social comedy rather than psychological tragedy. The final effect—of these stories and of the Mom novels—is meant to be wryly amusing rather than beautifully sad.

This feeling accounts for the first big choice I made when I planned the first Mom story, a choice that I carried over into the novels: Mom would be an armchair detective. She would never visit the scene of a crime, grill a suspect, or, God forbid, look at a corpse. All her inquiries into murder would take place at her own dinner table, between the chicken soup and the *schnecken*. Violent crime is outside the direct experience of most of us (knock wood!), but we are all familiar with the venal landlord, the crooked TV repairman, the good-for-nothing son-in-law, the beatendown wife, all these everyday, morally imperfect types that Mom uses as analogies in solving her son Dave's murder cases.

This then is the final phase of my developing ideas about the detective story. I see it now not only as an entertaining puzzle, not only as a showcase for a colorful larger-than-life character, but also as a dramatic commentary (sometimes, I hope, a witty one) on the vicissitudes of ordinary life, on what we're all up against in this world.

MY MOTHER, THE DETECTIVE

Mom's arena may be the kitchen, but that arena has a lot in common with the "mean streets" that her policeman son is forced to patrol. What they have in common is that funny, sad, messy phenomenon known as human nature.

Looking back on the stories in this volume, I have discovered a surprising thing. This organic approach to the detective story—in which everything, including the puzzle elements, relates to some central theme—is already part of several of them, notably "Mom in the Spring" and "Mom Sings an Aria." I just didn't realize it at the time, and therefore it took me twenty years to build on it.

So I think, in this final phase, that I have resolved the old conflict between my love of detective fiction and my love of realistic fiction.

I realize now that the world can be looked at in two ways. Realistic fiction draws us into the action, puts us behind the eyes of its characters, makes us feel their experience from the inside. But the world can also be looked at from the outside, as the detective story does. We can be observers as well as participants, members of the audience as well as actors on the stage; even as we become emotionally involved in the play and empathize with the characters, we can maintain that cool distance from them that the detective maintains from the subjects of his investigations. Life is something to plunge into, live to the full; but life is also a mystery to stand apart from, observe, investigate, solve.

It's pointless, therefore, to talk about one form being superior to the other. Each simply provides its own kind of understanding and pleasure.

And yet—though I am attracted to both ways of looking at the world, though I love both kinds of fiction—I confess that I will always have a special, and no doubt irrational, place in my affections for the detective story. It was, after all, my earliest love, and we all know that you never get over that one.

James Yaffe
Colorado Springs
September 1996

18

MOM KNOWS BEST

MY MOTHER ALWAYS WANTED ME TO BE A professional man. It didn't matter to her what kind of profession. Any kind would do, as long as it was really "professional," and absolutely not "business."

"Your uncles are in business, your cousins are in business, your Papa was in business, and none of them ever made a cent of money," Mom always said. "Except your Uncle Max, and he don't count, because God forbid you should ever turn out to be such a physical and nervous wreck as your Uncle Max and your Aunt Selma."

And so, even when I was a small boy in the Bronx, Mom saw to it that I got some professional training. She gave me chemistry sets for my birthday; she made me take violin lessons; she even encouraged me to work my childish charms on a cousin of ours who was a lawyer. And finally Mom got her wish. Today I am a professional man. But I'm afraid this fact has never given Mom any satisfaction. You see, she didn't exactly expect me to become a policeman.

From the very beginning she raised objections. All sorts of objections, every day a new objection but most of them were smokescreens. Her antagonism to the life of a policeman really boils down to two points. One: the work is dangerous. "All those gangsters and dope fiends and bookies and hatchet murderers and other such *goniffs* you have to deal with," she says. "Isn't it possible that you could get hurt some day?"

Two: she thinks the job is beneath me. "Always it was my ambition that you should take up something that needs a little intelligence and brainpower," she says. "But this detective work, this figuring out who killed who, and playing cops and robbers like the kiddies in the park, this is no work for a grown-up man. For all the brains it takes, believe me, you might as well be in business with your uncles."

MY MOTHER, THE DETECTIVE

And there is simply no way of talking Mom out of this opinion, of convincing her of the dignity and difficulty of my profession. Even though I've done pretty well for myself, even though I'm in plain-clothes now and chief assistant to Inspector Slattery, Mom still makes fun of me. And with justice. Because to tell the truth, this cops and robbers business is child's play—for Mom. Figuring out who killed who *is* an easy job—for Mom. With her ordinary common-sense, and her natural talent for seeing into people's motives and never letting herself be fooled by anybody (this talent comes from her long experience with shifty-eyed butchers and delicatessen store clerks), Mom is usually able to solve over the dinner table crimes that keep the police running around in circles for weeks.

In fact, I might even go so far as to say that my chief value to the Homicide Squad lies not in the strenuous investigating, manhunting, and third-degreeing that I do all week, but in the revealing conversations I have with Mom every Friday night, when she invites my wife and me up to the Bronx for dinner.

Take last Friday night, for instance.

Shirley and I got to Mom's apartment at six. Mom gave us the usual glass of wine, and we sat down to the usual roast chicken dinner (which is really unusual, because who can equal Mom's roast chicken?). For a while, the conversation ran along the usual lines. Mom told us about the ailments and scandals of everybody in the neighborhood. Then she gave Shirley advice on how to shop for groceries. Shirley is a Wellesley graduate with a degree in psychology and sociology, so naturally Mom is convinced that she's incapable of understanding the practical affairs of life. Then she lectured me on wrapping up warm in this damp weather. Finally, after bringing in the noodle soup, she asked me: "So how is the work going, Davie?"

"Nothing very interesting, Mom," I said. "Just an ordinary every-day murder case. Three suspects. One of them must be guilty. It's just a question of working on them long enough, till the guilty one cracks."

"And so far he didn't crack yet, the guilty party?"

"Not yet, Mom. But he will, all right. We'll sweat it out of him."

"And out of yourselves, while you're at it!" Mom gave a sigh. "This third degree, it's harder on the policemen than it is on the crooks. If you men only would stop a minute and use your heads, look at all the *tsouris* you'd save. Believe me, there isn't a single one of you that don't need a mother to look after you."

"It's not a question of using our heads, Mom. It's patience, pure patience. I'll tell you about this case, and you can judge for yourself. You see, this girl was killed in a hotel downtown. A sort of high-class low-class hotel, if you know what I mean. Very sporty, expensive crowd. Stage people, gamblers, radio and television people—a pretty flashy assortment. And blondes. The place is full of platinum blondes. With no visible means of support. Maybe they call themselves dancers—only they haven't stood on a chorus line for years; maybe they say they're models—only they never get any closer to a magazine cover than a million other readers.

"That's what this dead girl was. A genuine platinum blonde, who used the name Vilma Degrasse. Usual career—quit high school at sixteen to go on the chorus line. Quit the chorus line five years ago— to move into the hotel. Been living there ever since, in two rooms on the fifth floor. Her and a steady stream of admirers. All male—"

"And to make a long story short," Shirley cut in, "last night one of them killed her."

Shirley is always taking it on herself to make my long stories short. This doesn't bother me much—when I married Shirley, I knew I was getting a superior-type woman—but it never fails to get a rise out of Mom.

She rose now. "Well, now, isn't that interesting?" she said, turning to Shirley with a sweet polite smile. "So you're working on the case too, are you, Shirley dear?"

Shirley smiled right back at Mom, just as sweetly and politely. "Not at all, Mother. I'm just trying to help David cure himself of his terrible habit of talking on and on and never getting to the point. It's something he picked up in his childhood, though goodness knows from whom."

"Now here's our three suspects," I interrupted quickly, as I saw a gleam coming into Mom's eye. "At ten o'clock last night the girl was escorted into the lobby by a gentleman—middle-aged banker of this city named Griswold. Very unhappy about having his name mentioned in the papers. They were seen coming in by the clerk at the desk and by the elevator girl. The clerk is a gray-haired, seedy old man named Bigelow. The grumpy type. When I questioned him this afternoon he complained every two minutes about how he'd been standing on his feet behind that desk for four hours, and how the management don't even allow him to have a radio to help pass the time, and how the Assistant Manager is always poking around to make sure the clerks don't hide any magazines or newspapers under the desk, and so on and so on. And all the time this Bigelow was blowing beer fumes into my face. Unpleasant character, but just the same I think he's telling the truth. No apparent reason to lie.

"The elevator girl is Sadie Delaney, a talkative dark-haired Irish girl. Not married yet, built on the large side, but very cheerful and hearty, always doing special favors for people in the hotel. A good witness, too—cooperative and bright.

"So anyway, Sadie took the Degrasse girl and old Griswold up to the fifth floor, said good night to them, and rode down again. She passed the time with Bigelow about ten minutes, then she got a buzz from the fifth floor. She went up and found old Griswold waiting for the elevator and looking very mad. She took him down and said good night again, but he didn't answer her. He went stamping out of the lobby—"

At this moment there was an interruption as Shirley finished her noodle soup. "Oh, Mother, that soup was delicious," she said. "It's such a pleasure to taste your cooking. You know, that's really what you do *best* in the world."

"Thank you, with kindness, darling." Mom said. "But that's how it was with all the girls in my day, so I can't take any special credit. Even if we was too poor to go to college, we always learned something useful. We didn't fill our heads with a lot of *meshuggene* ideas that are no good to anybody—like so many of the young girls nowadays."

I saw that Shirley was getting ready to answer this, so I took a deep breath and hurtled on with my story:

"A minute later, enter Suspect Number Two. This is Tom Monahan, the hotel handyman. He was just going off duty, but he told Sadie that Miss Degrasse had called him earlier that day to fix a leak in her bathtub, and he was afraid she'd be mad if he didn't do it before she went to bed. So Sadie rode him up to the fifth floor and rode down again. No sooner did she get down than she heard another buzz from five. She went up again and found Tom. He said he had knocked on the girl's door, got no answer, so he figured she was asleep already. He'd fix the bathtub tomorrow. Down he went with Sadie, and straight home from there.

"Now Sadie and Bigelow chatted for about twenty minutes in the lobby. They talked about the big prizefight which was on that night, and how brutal it was, and what a beating the champ was taking. Their chat was interrupted by Suspect Number Three.

"This is young Artie Fellows, playboy about town, theatrical angel, and general no-good, who's been showing up to see the Degrasse girl a lot of nights this last month. He was in evening clothes. Just left a party at the home of his young fiancée that he's going to marry in June. Sadie rode him up to the fifth floor and left him there. Five minutes later, the buzzer started ringing loud and long. She rode up again and found Fellows looking green. He told her he'd just entered the girl's apartment with his key—the key she gave him—and found her lying dead on her bed. Well, the house dick was called, and a doctor and the police, and it was finally decided that somebody stunned her with a blow on the back of the head, administered by a bronze candlestick, her own property. And then, when she was stunned, this somebody smothered her to death with a pillow.

"We found the pillow on the floor next to the body. It was all rumpled up, and there were teeth marks and saliva stains to show what happened."

"Somehow," Shirley said, "I find it hard to feel much sympathy for a cheap unrefined girl like that. Usually such people get what they deserve."

"Not always," Mom said, in a musing voice, as if she were talking to herself. "There's plenty people running around in this world that maybe ought to get themselves smothered. Not enough to kill them maybe—just a little bit smothered, to teach them a lesson." Before Shirley could say a word to this, Mom turned to me very calmly and said, "So go on with the case, please."

"Well, the first thing we did, of course, was to question the three men. Here's what they tell us: Griswold was cagey at first, but finally he came out and admitted that he and the blonde had an argument after they got into her apartment. She told him she was through with him, she'd found another gentleman friend who was younger and richer—young Fellows most likely. Griswold says he was mad when he walked out, but claims he didn't kill her. Says he left her very much alive, turning on her television set to listen to the big prizefight. She was a great sports fan, especially if there was lots of blood. Well, so much for Griswold.

"For a while the handyman Tom Monahan looked like our murderer. We discovered a funny thing. There was absolutely nothing wrong with the bathtub in the Degrasse girl's apartment. So finally Monahan came out with the truth. He and the blonde were carrying on a little flirtation—he's a big husky, good-looking fellow, and she wasn't what you'd call particular. Monahan made up that bathtub dodge as an excuse to go up and see her. But he sticks to his story about knocking on the door and getting no answer. Incidentally, we asked him whether he heard the television going inside the room. He says he didn't notice.

"As for Artie Fellows—he still claims he came into the room and found her dead. What's more, he corroborates Griswold's story about the television. The television was on full blast when he came in, he says. In fact, this struck him as an especially gruesome touch, what with that blonde lying dead on the bed.

"So that's the set-up, Mom. It's got to be one of those three. It can't be anybody else who lives in the hotel, because we've checked up on everybody—it's a small hotel, not many tenants, and they've all got alibis. And it can't be anybody from the outside, because the clerk and the elevator girl didn't see anybody else come in or out. In other words, it's strictly a routine job. Griswold, Monahan, or Fellows, take your choice. Eeny-meeny-miney—!"

"You forgot Moe," Mom said. This remark struck me as slightly senseless, but I gave Mom a sharp look anyway—because her senseless remarks have a way of turning out to contain more sense than you'd expect. "What do you mean by that?"

"Never mind what I mean by that," she said. "Time for the chicken."

I was forced to control my curiosity while Mom served the chicken. When she finally got settled again in her place, I reminded her where we had broken off in our conversation.

"So now you've got those three men in your police station, is that it?" she said. "And you're beating them with rubber hoses?"

"Mom, how many times have I told you, we don't use rubber hoses. Modern police methods—"

"All right, all right, so you're psycho-annihilating them. Whatever it is, I'm positive it don't make no sense. The way you're handling things with this Platonic blonde—"

"*Platinum* blonde, Mother dear," Shirley said.

"So I said it." Mother gave Shirley a sharp look, then turned back to me.

"What's holding you up on this case, I'd like to know? Why are you wasting your time with third degrees? A bunch of *schlemiels*! Why don't you arrest the one that killed her?"

"Because we don't know the one that killed her! In a few hours—"

"A few hours, phooey! A few years is more like it, the way you're going. So stop using your fists and your lungs, and start using your brains. That's the big trouble with the world today, too many fists and lungs, not enough brains. Listen, I wouldn't be surprised if you never even bothered to ask yourself the four most important questions."

"What questions, Mom? We've asked a million of them."

"Eat your string beans, and I'll tell you. Conversation at the table is fine, but a young man has got to have his daily supply of green vegetables."

I blushed a little, as I always do when Mom treats me like a small boy in front of Shirley, but I obediently started in on my string beans. And Mom started in on her "four most important questions."

"The first question," she said, "This Tom Monahan, the handyman. Has he got a wife?"

"Mom, is that one of your mysterious questions? Why, that's the first thing we found out. No, he doesn't have a wife. So if you're looking for a jealousy angle, you'd better—"

"String beans!" Mom said, pointing her finger imperiously. "It's my turn now to do the thinking, please. If you don't mind, the second question. How come this Platonic blonde—"

"Platinum, Mother," Shirley said.

"Thank you, thank you," Mom said. "Such an advantage, isn't it, to have a daughter-in-law that speaks such good English and isn't afraid to let the whole world know about it. —So Davie, how come, I was asking, this *Platonic* blonde didn't have any lipstick on when she got killed?"

This question actually amazed me a little. "Mom, how did you know she didn't have any lipstick on? I didn't say anything about—"

"You said that the pillow she was smothered with had marks on it from teeth and saliva. But you didn't mention any lipstick marks. A lady gets a pillow over her face, believe me, she's going to leave lipstick marks as a result from the experience. Unless she didn't have any lipstick on! So how come she didn't?"

"I don't know how, Mom. She was getting ready to go to bed, so I suppose she washed her lipstick off. Is it really important?"

"Only to smart people," Mom said, patting me on the hand with a sweet smile. "The third question. When this playboy found her body, this Artie Fellows, the television was going full blast, is that right? So tell me, please, what program was on the television then?"

"Mom, are you crazy? Who cares what program was on the television? It's a murder we're investigating, not the television schedule—"

"In other words, you don't know what was on the television then?"

MOM KNOWS BEST

"As a matter of fact, I do know. Fellows happened to say so. A musical program, some concert orchestra playing classical music. He noticed it because the music was very soft and sad, and he says he'll always think of it as Vilma Degrasse's swan song. Very romantic, Mom, but will you tell me what the hell that's got to do—"

"Swearing I don't like," Mom said, quietly but firmly. "Such language you can use in your stationhouse with the other policemen, but in my home you'll talk like a gentleman."

"I'm sorry, Mom," I mumbled, avoiding Shirley's eye.

"Fourth and last question," Mom said. "This hotel where she got killed, it's not located in such a swanky neighborhood, is it?"

"Mom, what does it matter—?"

"Do you answer me, or don't you?"

"It's a mixed-up neighborhood. The block that this hotel is on is very swanky and modern-looking. But right around the corner is Third Avenue, with all those tenement houses and dirty little bars where the bums hang out. All right, Mrs. Sherlock, does that help you? Is that the significant piece in the jigsaw puzzle which makes everything else fit together?"

Mom smiled quickly, unperturbed by my sarcasm. "If you want to know—yes, it is."

My past experience with Mom was enough to make me start a little. But at the same time I just didn't see how she could possibly have solved the case on the little evidence I had given her. So I pretended to be unimpressed. "Well, let me in on it, why don't you? Which one of those men do you want me to book?"

"The answer to that," Mom said, with a smile of secret wisdom that infuriated me, "you'll find out in a minute."

"You mean, you really *know*—?"

"Why shouldn't I know? I know how people act, don't I? Just because it's a murder case, that don't mean people are all of a sudden going to stop acting like people. A girl like that Platonic blonde—"

"Platinum," Shirley murmured under her breath—evidently just for the principle of the thing, because Mom ignored her elaborately.

"—a girl who all her life is around men, such a girl is very fussy

27

how she looks when a man drops in. So how come, when you found her dead, she didn't have any lipstick on? When Suspect Number One, this banker, this Mr. Grizzly—"

"Griswold! Just as I suspected!" I cried.

But Mom ignored me and went on, "When he brought her home, she had lipstick on. He took her up to her apartment, she told him she wouldn't go out with him any more, she laughed at him and sent him away—do you think she took her lipstick off before he left? Believe me, it's impossible. When a woman is making a fool out of a man, *that's* when she wants to look absolutely at her best! So when Suspect Number One went away, she was still alive—with her lipstick on."

"Well—it sounds reasonable. So it was Suspect Number Two who did it, then. Tom Monahan! I had a feeling—"

"That's a lovely feeling," Mom said. "Too bad it don't have any connection with the truth. This Tom Monahan knocked on the door and asked her if he could come in and see her. A handsome young fellow that she was flirting with—listen, even if she already took her lipstick off for the night, you can bet she never would've let him through the door without putting it right back on again. But she *didn't* put it right back on again. So that means she didn't let him through the door. For some reason she didn't hear his knock—maybe because the television was on too loud. Anyway, he couldn't have killed her."

"And that leaves Suspect Number Three," I said. "Artie Fellows. I had a hunch it was him all along. Your lipstick clue won't work for him. He had a key to the apartment. She might've been in bed already, with her lipstick off, when all of a sudden he came barging in with his key."

"Maybe so," Mom said. "But you could get a big headache trying to prove it. You remember, I asked you that question, what was on the television when Suspect Number Three found the body? Earlier in the evening, when Suspect Number One went away, the girl turned on the big prizefight. But it was an hour later before Suspect Number Three showed up. The fight must be over by then— especially a fight that was so uneven. Like the clerk and the elevator girl said, the champion was taking a terrible beating. So the fight was over, but the television was still on when Suspect Number Three found the body. Why?"

"That's a tough one, Mom. Maybe because she wanted to watch the program that came on after the fight."

"Maybe, maybe not. So what program was she watching? A concert orchestra, playing classical music! Now I ask you, Davie, from everything you know about this girl—a chorus girl that never even finished high school—does she sound like the type that's interested in classical music? Not to me she don't. So why did she still leave the television on? Only one answer. Because she was killed while the prizefight was still going, and naturally she couldn't turn off the television after she was dead. So there you are—it couldn't be Suspect Number Three, since he got there too late."

"But, Mom, don't you realize what you're saying? It couldn't be any of the three Suspects, because you just proved it— and it couldn't be anybody else from outside, because the clerk and the elevator girl were watching the lobby—and we know it couldn't be anybody else in the building, because everyone has an alibi. In other words, it couldn't be anybody!"

"Alibi!" Mom gave a contemptuous little shrug. "Listen, Davie, when you get to be as old as me, you'll find out that the world is full of Alibi Jakes." ("Ikes," Shirley muttered.) "Nothing is easier than tripping up an Alibi Jake. People doing favors for other people, for instance. Take your Aunt Selma's cook—"

"For Pete's sake, Mom, what possible connection could there be between Aunt Selma's cook and—"

"For six whole months, every night your Aunt Selma's cook sneaked out of the apartment to meet the delivery man from the grocery store. All the time your Aunt Selma's chambermaid knew it —but did she tell your Aunt Selma? Not a word. Every time your Aunt Selma rang for the cook, the chambermaid answered the bell. The cook is busy baking a cake, she said, or the cook has a spitting headache, or the cook is arguing over the phone with the butcher— or some excuse. Davie, you don't know servants like I do. As long as they're not mad at each other, they got a way of sticking together. Especially when it's a question of fooling the boss."

A small glimmer of understanding was beginning to come to me. "Mom, what are you getting at exactly?"

"You don't know yet? What a *nebbish* son I've got!"

"Well, if I'm not mistaken, you could be talking about the clerk and Sadie the elevator girl."

"A genius! A regular Dr. Einstein! Naturally that's who I'm talking about. You told me yourself, how this elevator girl is so obliging and good-natured, and always doing special favors for people. Well, there was twenty minutes *after* Suspect Number Two went away and *before* Suspect Number Three went up in the elevator, and during those twenty minutes this clerk and this elevator girl were supposed to be chatting together about the prizefight on television, how brutal it was and what a beating the champion was getting. But what I'd like to know is—"

I couldn't keep myself from blurting it out. "How did Bigelow know the fight was so brutal if he was standing behind his desk all night since there's no television or even radio in the lobby? That's what you're getting at, isn't it, Mom? You're saying that after Tom Monahan left and before Artie Fellows arrived, Bigelow came out from behind his desk, took the elevator up to the fifth floor, and killed the Degrasse girl—and while he was killing her, he saw the prizefight on the television in her room! And all this time, Sadie stayed downstairs and watched the desk for him, and covered up for him because she's so good-natured!"

I was extremely pleased with myself for catching on so quickly, and it surprised me when Mom gave an annoyed sigh. "Good-natured," she said, "how good-natured can a person be? Is anybody so good-natured that they'd give a man an alibi for a murder? They might be willing to give him an alibi if he slipped away from the desk for *another* reason—but not for a murder."

"But, Mom, you yourself suggested—*what* other reason?"

"You told me the reason yourself," Mom said. "You just don't pay attention, Davie, not even to your own words. You explained to me how you questioned the clerk this afternoon, and how he complained to you every two minutes that he'd been standing behind his desk for four hours, and how he blew beer fumes in your face. So if he'd been standing behind his desk for four hours, and the Assistant Manager was always poking around to see he wasn't hiding anything under it, so where did he get a drink of beer?"

This question stunned me. I couldn't say a word.

"This is why I asked you about the neighborhood," Mom said. "And you told me what I thought already. Around the corner is Third Avenue. Along Third Avenue is lots of bars. So this is how the clerk got his beer—he sneaked around the corner a few times to one of those bars. Chances are he does it every day—and chances are it's what he did last night, when he and the elevator girl were supposed to be chatting. And she gave him an alibi because she didn't want him to lose his job."

"Very clever deduction, Mother," Shirley said. "But what use is it to David? You know, he can't arrest a man for taking a drink during working hours."

"Oh, thank you very much for the information," Mother said, giving Shirley her most condescending smile. "But who wants to arrest him? Davie, don't it even pop into your head yet? If the clerk was off in a bar somewhere drinking beer, who's to prove where the elevator girl was?"

"Sadie? Why, she was in the lobby chatting with—" I stopped short, as the truth dawned on me at last. "Of course, of course! That conversation she had with Bigelow about the prizefight! It takes two people to make a conversation! The same question I asked for Bigelow also goes for Sadie. How did she know that the fight was so brutal and that the champion was taking such a licking? She must've seen it on television—on the blonde's television!"

"Finally you're talking like a slightly intelligent human being," Mom said, beaming with motherly pride, despite her sarcastic words. "While the clerk was away in his bar, this elevator girl went up to the fifth floor, knocked on the blonde's door, then went into the room and killed her. And incidentally, you can see now why the blonde didn't bother to put her lipstick on when the elevator girl knocked. Because naturally she wouldn't care how she looked in front of an elevator girl."

31

"But what about the motive, Mom? What was Sadie's motive?"

"Motive? The easiest part. Why do you think I asked you if this handyman, Tom Monahan, was married? A good-looking unmarried Irish boy—a good-natured unmarried Irish girl—and a blonde who's coming between them. Listen, I'd be surprised if such a situation *didn't* end up in murder!"

Well, I spent the next few minutes apologizing to Mom for my skepticism—while Shirley put on a distant, faraway look, as if she were completely indifferent to what was going on, and not the least bit annoyed or jealous at Mom's triumph.

But one little thing still gnawed at me, and finally I came out with it.

"Mom, I'm still puzzled about Bigelow, the clerk. He and Sadie both spoke about how brutal the fight was, just as if they'd seen it on television. We know now how Sadie got to see the fight—on the television set in the blonde's room. But how did Bigelow get to see it, Mom? —unless he was up in the blonde's room, too?"

"Davie, Davie, my little baby," Mom said, with a rather fond smile. "You forgot already where this Bigelow was for twenty minutes. In a bar drinking beer. And these days—though naturally I don't patronize such places myself—I hear that you can't get a beer in any bar without getting, along with it—"

"Television!" I cried. Then I jumped to my feet. "Mom, you're a mastermind! I'll call up headquarters right now, and tell the Inspector!"

But Mom's voice, quiet and firm, made me sink back into my seat. "Such *chutzpah!*" she said. "Nobody's calling up anywhere, or telling anything to anybody, till he finishes his string beans!"

MOM MAKES A BET

EVEN THOUGH I'VE BEEN WORKING FOR THE NEW York Homicide Squad almost five years, I still give a little shudder at the thought that some day somebody might discover my secret—specifically, that most of my successful cases were really solved by my mother. As a matter of fact, this is one of Mom's greatest weapons against me. Whenever she wants me to give up an afternoon to fix her icebox, or to find an eligible young policeman for one of her unmarried nieces, or to take her part in an argument with my wife Shirley, Mom always remarks, in an innocent, casual tone of voice, "Wouldn't they give a big horse laugh, Davie, those other young fellows on the Homicide Squad, if somebody told them how you figured out what happened to that old lady that was dropped down the laundry chute in that midtown hotel?"

A hundred times in the last five years I have resolved that I would never tell Mom about any of my cases again. And a hundred times —under the influence of Mom's delicious roast chicken, and her sharp commanding look that turns me into a little boy again—I have broken my own resolution. "And incidentally," Mom herself would probably add, if she read that last sentence, "you're not exactly dying with unhappiness, are you, when Inspector Slattery gives you a slap on the back, and tells you what a budding young Sherlock you are?"

That's the wonderful thing about Mom. She understands human psychology—a little too well for comfort.

Anyway, last Friday night Shirley and I had dinner in the Bronx as usual, and as soon as we had settled down to our chopped liver Mom asked me her usual question: "So, Davie, how is the work going these days?"

"Nothing very exciting, Mom. I'm on a case now which is strictly open-and-shut. We know who the murderer is, and we're bound to get a conviction."

"Why, then, do you have such a gloomy look on your face? Like your Uncle Nathan you look, when he found out that his *schnorrer* brother-in-law Seymour was coming to visit him."

"Well, frankly, Mom, there is something about this case, I can't exactly put my finger on it. It's just that—well, usually when you arrest a murderer, you feel very pleased with yourself. You say to yourself, 'There's one more rat out of circulation.' But, somehow, this murderer that we arrested yesterday—well, he's such a nice old gentleman—"

"Sentimentality, pure sentimentality," Shirley said, giving me one of her pitying sighs. Shirley majored in sociology and psychology at Wellesley, so naturally she's a very superior girl, and I ought to feel honored by her pity. "How many times have I told you, David, if Inspector Slattery is satisfied with a case, then you mustn't stick your nose in out of sheer sentimentality. That's not the way a person gets ahead in this world—"

"I agree," Mom said, with a sweet smile at Shirley. "People shouldn't stick their noses in. It's a subject I've been meaning to bring up—"

"Let me tell you about this case, Mom," I said quickly, because Mom's chopped liver should be enjoyed in an atmosphere of peace and harmony. Sure enough, Mom's curiosity about the case was the one thing that could sidetrack her from defending me against my wife —and so, I went right into the story.

"There's a delicatessen downtown," I said, "called Krumholz' Sixth Avenue Grotto—a very well-known little place, it gets a big crowd of celebrities, theatrical people, athletes, and so on. At night the place is usually crowded, but business is lighter during the lunch hour.

"So yesterday, at lunch, this theatrical producer, DeWitt Grady, went to Krumholz' Grotto with his father-in-law, old Dr. Bartlett, the famous surgeon, now retired. Grady was one of the Grotto's regular customers. He came in there three or four times every week, and was known and disliked by all the employees. From all reports, he was a terribly overbearing, bad-mannered, nasty person, this Grady, always making complaints and throwing his weight around."

MOM MAKES A BET

"It's one of the primary traits of theatrical people," Shirley said. "Sociological studies prove that the average theatrical person—"

"Tell me, darling," Mom said to Shirley, "did anybody ever make a sophie-logical study of sophie-logical people?"

"I don't follow you, Mother," Shirley said, "What exactly are you driving at?"

"Grady was especially obnoxious," I cut in, "to one of the waiters in the Grotto, a little old man named Irving. Now, Irving has been working for Krumholz for 30 years, and everybody knows him and likes him, because he's so sweet and good-natured, always asking the customers about their illnesses and their babies, and remembering, their birthdays and anniversaries, and so on. Maybe that was why Grady took such particular pleasure in picking on Irving. Anyway, whenever he came to the Grotto, Grady made Irving's life miserable. He ordered him around in a high-handed tone. He made insulting remarks and sarcastic jokes. He sneered at the old man and humiliated him, and sometimes didn't even leave him a tip.

"Yesterday afternoon, during lunch, was no exception. Grady and his father-in-law, Dr. Bartlett, sat down at one of Irving's tables, and right away Grady started in. He called Irving over with some remark about 'if your legs can carry you this far, old man.' He ordered the first course—Blue Point oysters—and told Irving not to be stingy with the horseradish. Krumholz' Grotto is famous for its horseradish, you know—'the strongest horseradish in town,' that's one of its slogans—and Grady liked to accuse Irving of cheating the customers out of their horseradish.

"Then, when Irving brought the oysters, Grady ordered a couple of bowls of noodle soup, for Dr. Bartlett and himself. And he told Irving to be sure that his own noodle soup had no salt. 'I was just to the doctor last week,' Grady said, 'and he told me if I eat more salt I'll get a terrible heartburn.' Half a dozen times Grady repeated these instructions to Irving, and Irving assured him that there wouldn't be any salt in his noodle soup, and Grady said, 'I can't trust you. You'll forget to tell the cook. You're losing your memory, old man.' So Grady called over Krumholz, and told him to check up on Irving and make sure that one of the noodle soups didn't have any salt in it

—and you can imagine how humiliating this must have been for poor old Irving. Well, at last Irving went out to the kitchen for the noodle soup—with Grady yelling after him, 'And for Pete's sake, be careful, don't stick your thumb in it!' "

"This Grady," Mom said, "he reminds me of a cousin of your late father."

At this Shirley gave a superior little laugh. "Really, Mother, it's amusing how everybody in the world reminds you of somebody you know."

"This is because I know a lot of people," Mom answered, without batting an eyelash. "My knowledge of people don't come strictly out of books. It's the difference between somebody that actually plays in the gin rummy game, and somebody that only sits around and *kibitzes*."

"As I was saying," I broke in, "Irving went out to the kitchen, told Looie the cook to give him two noodle soups, and warned him several times that one of the soups shouldn't have any salt in it. So Looie poured out one bowl from the big vat where the noodle soup, all salted and ready to serve, was kept. The other bowl he mixed up and cooked specially himself, leaving out the salt. Then the two bowls of soup were placed on Irving's tray, and Irving started out of the kitchen. At the swinging door which led from the kitchen to the main dining-room, Krumholz himself was standing. Grady being such a steady customer, Krumholz wasn't going to take any chances with Grady's order. So Krumholz stopped Irving, dipped a spoon into Grady's soup, and swallowed a whole spoonful of it himself, just to make sure that there wasn't any salt in it. Don't forget that, Mom, because it's very important. Krumholz actually tasted Grady's soup. He found that it tasted fine, and there wasn't any salt in it, so he told Irving to go ahead and serve it.

"That's what Irving did. He carried his tray directly across the dining-room to the table where Grady and Dr. Bartlett were sitting. Even though Irving had several other people's orders on that same tray—a couple of bottles of beer, a big tall Krumholz Special Peach Sundae topped with whipped cream, and a piece of nesselrode pie—he went straight to Grady before anyone else. That's how scared poor Irving was of that Grady. He gave Grady and Dr. Bartlett their soup, Grady took a spoonful of it, smacked his lips, and said, 'It's not bad.' But that's as far as he got. Because he suddenly gave a groan and slumped to the floor, and by the time anybody could reach him he was dead. The Medical Examiner found a dose of potassium cyanide in him—and enough of it left over in the noodle soup to kill twenty more theatrical producers.

"And there you are, Mom. There was a bottle of potassium cyanide in the kitchen—Looie the cook kept it there to kill rats. He kept it locked up in a cupboard, but any one of Krumholz' employees had access to the key. So in the ordinary course of things we'd be faced with such a wide choice of suspects that we might never solve the case. Except for one little stroke of luck. Krumholz himself tasted Grady's noodle soup just before it was served. He drank a whole spoonful of it, and nothing happened to him. Therefore, the poison must have been put in the soup *after* it left the kitchen and *before* it got to Grady. And there was only one person who had the opportunity to put it there during that period of time—Irving the waiter. Poor old Irving." And as I came to the end of my story, I couldn't help giving a little sigh.

"Only you don't feel so happy about it, Davie," Mom said, in a voice which was almost gentle.

"It's the motive that bothers me, Mom," I said. "Is it possible that a man would really commit murder because someone accused him of putting his thumb in the soup? Honestly, that's carrying professional pride a little too far. Besides, this Irving—he just isn't the vindictive type. I've never seen such a nice, mild-mannered old man. You know, we had a terrible time taking his fingerprints down at the station—because after he dipped his fingers in the ink, he was afraid he'd get the desk sergeant's shirt cuffs dirty." I broke off with a shake of my head, a little angry at myself, and also noticing the look that Shirley was giving me. "I don't know what I'm getting all worked up about! The man committed murder, and he's going to pay the penalty, and that's all there is to it!"

After looking at me a moment with an expression that was half-affectionate and half-laughing in my face, Mom gave a sigh of her own. "Davie, Davie, so full of a kind heart and feeling sorry for people! Don't you know yet? Feeling sorry is no good to anybody, feeling sorry don't keep that old man out of the electric chair, feeling sorry don't find out who put the Potash and Cyanide in the soup—"

"Potassium, Mother dear," Shirley said. It was one of the delights of Shirley's life, the occasional little liberties that Mom took with the English language. Personally I never noticed them any more myself. After 33 years with Mom, my mind automatically makes the translation from "potash" to "potassium." But not Shirley. She never lets a single slip go by. What else is a Wellesley education for? "Po-tas-si-um," she repeated. "You spell that p-o-t-a-"

"Thank you, thank you, Shirley darling," Mom said, with a terribly polite wave of a chicken bone. "A regular little spelling bee you're turning into." Then Mom looked right back at me. "Like I was saying, before interruptions, better than a kind heart any day is brains. How about your brains, Davie? Along with the gun and the badge, don't the Homicide Squad issue you some brains maybe?"

"I'm afraid brains won't be much help to old Irving, Mom. It's an open-and-shut case."

"So let's open and shut it a little more. For instance, I notice that there's some important pieces of information you forgot to mention to me. Probably it's just an absent mind, no doubt *you* meant to mention them already—"

"What pieces of information, Mom? I've told you everything that's important,"

"About the motive you told me? Excuse me, I didn't hear it. Maybe I'm getting a little deaf in my old age—"

"I told you that I wasn't satisfied with Irving's motive, Mom—"

"Irving's motive? Who's talking from Irving's motive? What about everybody else's motive? What about the father-in-law, Dr. Bartlett—did he collect any money from this Grady's murder? What about Looie the cook—did he hate this Grady because Grady insulted his cooking? What about all that?"

Well, it always gives me a great deal of pleasure to triumph over Mom. The fact is, I get so few opportunities—so I try to make the most out of any one that comes along. "Well, well, Mom, I guess we stupid policemen are just a little bit ahead of you on this point," I said, puffing out my chest and putting on my most professional smirk. "Dr. Bartlett couldn't have killed Grady for his money, because Grady didn't have any money. He was almost broke. His last three shows were big flops, and he was living entirely on bluff. Besides which, Dr. Bartlett is a very rich man himself, with a Park Avenue penthouse. And Looie couldn't have killed Grady for insulting his cooking, because Grady *liked* Looie's cooking. In fact, the only person in the restaurant that Grady *never* insulted was Looie. He gave Looie big tips every month, and he used Looie as a caterer for all his parties. So I'm afraid your deductions were just a little inaccurate that time, Mom."

Strangely enough, Mom didn't look the least bit taken aback. She simply nodded her head and said, "Good. Exactly what I was thinking. Another point, Davie, and this is a big point, so think hard, please. What was it, please, that this Grady ordered to eat after his noodle soup?"

"What's that, Mom?"

"*After* his noodle soup, what did he order? You don't understand plain simple-minded English?"

"Mom, will you please tell me what difference it makes what he ordered *after* his noodle soup? He didn't eat it, Mom. It was the noodle soup that poisoned him, not—"

Mom gave a secret little smile. "I'm interested, this is what difference it makes. So humor a poor old woman that's getting soft in her head and answer the question please."

"All right, Mom, all right," I said. And to myself I thought: Women are all the same; even in the middle of a murder case they can't get their minds off irrelevant little details like food and housekeeping— "I don't remember exactly, but I did glance at the order check that Irving filled out, and I think Grady ordered a Krumholz Special Three-Decker Pinochle Sandwich. That's bacon, lettuce, mayonnaise, smoked herring, Russian dressing, and salami, with a pickle on the side."

"Thank you," Mom said. "This is a *very* important piece information." Shirley gave a sigh, and another one of her pitying looks, but Mom just smiled and went on, "The last, and final, important point. This Irving the waiter, he's such an old man. So how did he keep up with his work? In the rush hours, for instance, didn't he have trouble with the orders? Wasn't it hard for him to hold the trays? Explain, please."

"This is supposed to be an important point, Mom?"

"Maybe not to policemen and sophie-ologists," Mom said, with a smile, "but to ordinary common-sense people, absolutely it's important."

"If you say so, Mom. Well, it happens you're right, Irving *was* having trouble with his work. That's one of the most pitiful things about this whole case. The poor old man was getting much too old to be a waiter. He couldn't carry a heavy tray over his head with one hand any more, and this meant that it was almost impossible for him to weave his way in and out of the crowd during rush hours. So at the end of this month, Krumholz was planning to give him a surprise. He was planning to retire the old man, with a big bonus and a pension. In other words, Mom, if poor Irving could only have held out against Grady's insults for a few more weeks, he would've been free of them forever." I shook my head. "It's a sad case, Mom, a very sad case."

Mom shook her head back and forth, and said, "Oh, yes, a sad case, a sad sad case," and for a moment I had a slight suspicion that she was making fun of me. Then her head snapped up and she produced a huge magnificent snort of contempt—and believe me, this is one accomplishment of which Mom is a master. "Sad? It's a tragedy! We should have a funeral over it! And it should be followed by a *minyan*! Not for this Irving—for the police department, that can't see in front of its face its own nose! Irving I'm not worried about— Irving will be out of jail tomorrow—"

"Mom, what are you talking about? Nobody can do anything for Irving! He's—"

"*I* can do something for Irving. I can prove to you he didn't do the murder, and I can show you who did."

"I don't believe it, Mom."

40

She lifted her chin, very dignified. "So how much do you wish to bet? I'm needing some new wallpaper for my bedroom. If I do what I said, you'll come Sunday and put it up for me?"

"But Mom, Shirley was going to take me to the Metropolitan Museum of Art on Sunday. Sunday is the day Shirley exposes me to culture."

"Culture can wait. If I show you who's the murderer, you'll expose yourself to my wallpaper?"

I hesitated just a moment, then Shirley spoke, "Go ahead, David. You surely don't think you're going to lose."

I nodded. "All right, Mom, it's a bet." Mom reached across the table and shook my hand. Then she leaned back, put a big satisfied smile on her face, and said, "So now, here's the solution. First of all, I prove to you that Irving *couldn't* be the poisoner. It's the third important point I mentioned. Irving is an old man, you said. He can't do his job so good no more, you said. Especially he can't lift a heavy tray with one hand no more—both hands he needs, you said. All right, so yesterday for lunch, when he brought the noodle soup to this Grady, did he bring it on a heavy tray or a light tray? On a heavy tray—you told me it yourself. On the same tray with the two noodle soups, you said, was also two bottles beer, a Krumholz Special Peach Sundae, and a nesselrode pie. Not only a heavy tray, but a tray full of bottles and bowls and liquids and things that could spill and splash all over the place. Believe me, an old man like that Irving, who was already worried that he might make a mistake that this Grady could laugh at him for—believe me, this was one tray he was holding on to for dear life with two hands! And if he was holding on to it with two hands—"

"—then how was he able to drop the poison in the soup!" I said.

Mom nodded. "Exactly. Isn't it wonderful, what a brilliant son I got—when his mother does the thinking?"

I frowned a moment, thinking it over. Then I began to shake my head. "But, Mom, it's impossible. If Irving didn't put the poison in the soup, who did? Nobody else could have got at that soup while Irving was carrying it over to the table. And nobody could have got

41

at it after Irving set it down in front of Grady, because Grady started eating it right away."

"So what about before the soup left the kitchen?"

"But that's even more impossible, Mom. Because Krumholz stood at the kitchen door and drank a whole spoonful of that soup—"

"Maybe," Mom said, raising a finger mysteriously. "And also, maybe not." She smiled around the table a moment, getting the most out of her scene, and then she went on, "This brings me to another one of my important points. What did this Grady order *after* his noodle soup? I asked you. A Krumholz Three Decker Pinochle Club Sandwich, you answered me. With bacon, with mayonnaise, with Russian dressing, with smoked herring, with salami. So I ask you, Davie—isn't this a little peculiar maybe?"

"Well, I think a man is crazy to eat a thing like that, Mom, but otherwise it doesn't strike me as particularly—"

"Davie, Davie. One minute this Grady says to Irving, don't put any salt in my noodle soup, the doctor says I'll get a bad heartburn if I eat salt. And the next minute, he orders a sandwich with bacon, mayonnaise, smoked herring, Russian dressing, *and* salami—things which are absolutely full of salt! In fact, a sandwich like that, it's practically a salt mine!"

"Yes, Mom, I see what you mean. It *is* peculiar. But why—"

"Only one reason why. He was lying, Davie. When he said he didn't want no salt in his soup because of his heartburn, he was telling a big lie. What he wanted only was to be sure that Looie the cook should make one specific, particular, *special* soup for him and another one for his father-in-law, Dr. Bartlett, and that Irving shouldn't possibly get them mixed up and give Dr. Bartlett's soup to him and his soup to Dr. Bartlett. So to make sure of this, he tells this lie about wanting a bowl of soup that don't have no salt in it."

"But why, Mom? Why should Grady have cared which bowl of soup got to him and which one got to Dr. Bartlett?"

"Because, Davie, this Grady didn't want by accident to get the bowl of soup that Looie the cook put the Potash and Cyanide into."

For a second my confusion was great, and I merely gaped. I seem to spend a great deal of my time with Mom, merely gaping. Finally

I got hold of myself and said, "Mom, do you mean—that Grady and Looie—"

"Not only do I mean this, but it's the only thing I could mean. Dr. Bartlett didn't have no motive to kill this Grady. But such a motive did Grady have to kill Dr. Bartlett! Grady was broke, Dr. Bartlett was a man with a Park Avenue penthouse, Dr. Bartlett dies, his daughter Mrs. Grady no doubt collects all the money, plus the Park Avenue penthouse, and Grady can put on some more flops again. A perfect motive! And who should he have for a partner in this murder? Who was it that made the soup in the first place, so he could make absolutely sure that the poison got into the right bowl? Who was it that was a big favorite with this Grady, that got big tips from him and catered at his parties? Who was it that could get to the rat poison with no trouble at all? Looie the cook—who else?"

I nodded my head enthusiastically. "Yes, Mom, you're right, he was the only one—" I stopped short. "But Mom," I said, "it's impossible! Looie *can't* be guilty. First of all, it wasn't Dr. Bartlett's soup —the soup with salt in it—that got poisoned, it was Grady's soup— the soup *without* salt in it. And second of all, Krumholz himself tasted that bowl of soup—"

"Both these problems," Mom said, "have got the same answer."

"What is it, Mom? I don't see it."

"What is it? It's what I said before. This Grady reminds me of a cousin of your late father. His cousin Sadie Schwartz to be exact."

"Did *she* get poisoned too, Mom?"

"No, she didn't get poisoned. The resemblance is strictly a matter from personality. Is a murder case a special department in life? It's like everything else—it's people's personalities that count. Your father's cousin Sadie Schwartz, such an aggravation she was! A regular *schmendrick*! Nothing satisfied her, always yelling at people, always saying insulting things. The rest of the family, they wouldn't stand for it, they yelled at her and said insulting things right back at her. Believe me, I could tell about one time when I myself—and usually I'm a perfect lady—but this is outside of the point. The point is, what about those poor *schlimazls* who weren't in a position they could yell and insult right back at her? What about the people that depended on her, that made money from her, that sold her things? So how did *these* people get their revenge on cousin Sadie? Well, Davie, it's always the case in life. The worm turns—but he turns like a worm does, not like a man does. He turns in a *little* way, underground, so you couldn't hardly notice he was turning. When a worm wants to get his revenge on somebody, he don't make a lot of *big* trouble for that somebody, like shooting a hole in his head—he makes some kind of little, annoying, minor trouble, which sometimes is even worse than a hole in the head. Like Cousin Sadie—"

"Mom, will you *please* get to the point!"

"Cousin Sadie and the plumber," Mom repeated, with a sharp look. "For months and months, Cousin Sadie was getting on the nerves of the plumber. And why not? A woman with a voice like that, she'd get on a rabbi's nerves. So what does the plumber do, when Cousin Sadie yells at him because he didn't fix the pipes right? Does he knock her skull in with a wrench? Absolutely not. He gets his revenge in a *little* way. He smiles and bows and says, 'Yes, ma'am, I'll fix the pipes over again.' And then he fixes them so that from then on, at 12 o'clock midnight every night, for one whole hour, cousin Sadie's pipes start to give a bang!—bang! bang! bang!—for one whole hour, and is absolutely nothing nobody can do about it! For two months cousin Sadie don't get to sleep at night until after 1 o'clock—"

"Mom," I said, my voice getting a little hoarse by now, "what has this got to do with the murder case—?"

"This Grady," Mom says, "he reminds me of cousin Sadie. And Irving the waiter, he reminds me of the plumber. Does Irving get his revenge on this Grady in a big way—no, he don't. In a *little* way he gets it. He's a poor old man, but he's not so poor or so old that he can't get his revenge. This Grady tells him that he can't have salt in the soup. He tells him that if he has any salt he'll get a bad heartburn. So Irving says to himself, 'All right, so this is how it's going to be. Do you insult me and accuse me of putting my thumb in the soup? All right, so I'll *give* you your heartburn.' "

"I get it, Mom, I get it! " I cried. "Looie the cook put the poison in Dr. Bartlett's soup, after he poured it out of the vat. The soup that

Krumholz tasted at the kitchen door wasn't Dr. Bartlett's soup, it was the soup that Looie made specially. It was Grady's soup—so naturally Krumholz wasn't poisoned. But when Irving brought the order to the table, he *switched* soups! He gave Dr. Bartlett the soup that was meant for Grady, and he gave Grady the soup that was meant for Dr. Bartlett. In this way, he thought that he was going to give Grady a case of heartburn and without knowing it, he *killed* him!"

Mom settled back in her chair with a deep sigh. "Believe me, Davie," she said, "I couldn't have said it better myself. —And don't forget," she added, "I'm expecting you up here Sunday, to put up that wallpaper."

"Just a moment, Mother," Shirley said. "I'm afraid I'm not satisfied. I'm afraid there's one little loophole which completely destroys your theory."

"So?" Mom said, cocking her head forward with polite curiosity.

"Everything you say is based on the assumption that the old waiter—Irving, is that his name?—switched the two bowls of soup so that the murdered man would get the one with salt. Am I correct?"

Mom nodded.

"But how, Mother dear," and in spite of her polite tone, I could see the little gleam of anticipation in Shirley's eye, "how did Irving hope to get away with this scheme? Didn't he realize—how could he *help* but realize—that as soon as the victim tasted the soup and discovered that there was salt in it, he wouldn't eat another spoonful? Therefore, he *wouldn't* get heartburn, and Irving would merely have succeeded in making trouble for himself. Now then, Mother, how do you explain *that*?"

Mom folded her arms across *her* chest and smiled back at Shirley just as confidently. "I explain it, Shirley darling, in two words. Horse. Radish. Before he got the soup, Grady finished an order of Blue Point oysters with horseradish—Krumholz's famous horseradish—the strongest horseradish in New York, like the slogan says. So believe me, Irving knew that Grady wouldn't be able to taste whether his soup had salt in it or not. After you eat the strongest horseradish in New York, believe me, you don't taste *anything*!"

45

Shirley sank back a little, with an astounded scowl on her face, and Mom turned to me calmly. "Sunday morning, Davie," she said. "Don't forget."

"But you certainly didn't *mean* that ridiculous bet, Mother," Shirley said, attempting a casual laugh. "You certainly don't intend to stand in the way of David's cultural development."

"Make it early," Mom said, without even looking at Shirley.

And frankly, I wasn't sorry. The Metropolitan Museum of Art always ruins my feet, anyway.

MOM IN THE SPRING

IT WAS REALLY A BEAUTIFUL SPRING. I guess that's why it occurred to my wife Shirley and me that my mother ought to get married again.

"After all," I said, "the early fifties isn't so old. Why, Mom is livelier than the average girl of thirty. And I hate to think of her all alone, up there in that apartment in the Bronx."

"All right," said Shirley with a woman's usual brisk, businesslike approach to such matters, "who will we introduce her to?"

There was one inevitable answer to that question. Inspector Millner, of course. He was the oldest and most eligible bachelor on the Homicide Squad—that's my job, by the way, I'm a detective with Homicide—and he had all the right qualifications. He wasn't too bad-looking—sort of tall, thin, and awkward maybe, but Mom would like that much better than the slick, greasy, overgroomed type. In manner he was rather mournful and shy and unassertive—which would give Mom plenty of opportunity to manage him and baby him in turn. He was Jewish—Mom wouldn't feel comfortable with a man who wasn't Jewish. How could such a man understand her jokes? Best of all, he and Mom had an interest in common. Crime, that is. For I can hardly begin to count up all the murder cases which Mom has solved for me over the dinner table on Friday nights.

"So what's the first step?" I said to Shirley.

The first step, apparently, was to bring the romantic couple together. For this purpose a little innocent lying was necessary. Mom was told that Inspector Millner was a poor lonely bachelor who was sick of restaurant food, and dying to taste one of her home-cooked dinners. Inspector Millner was told that Mom was a poor lonely widow who was sick of cooking for herself and dying to show off her pot-roast to a nice appreciative gentleman. The upshot was, the

47

following Friday night Shirley and I brought Inspector Millner up to the Bronx with us for dinner.

We were a little worried about the impression that Mom would make on him. Mom is such a blunt, direct sort of person, sometimes she upsets people who aren't used to her. If the President of the United States himself were coming to dinner, I believe that Mom would receive him in the same plain house dress, feed him the same noodle soup, and tell him her opinion of his administration in the same sharp, sarcastic manner.

Well, right from the start Shirley and I were pleasantly surprised. Inspector Millner wasn't the President. From Mom's point of view, he was much better than the President. He was a shy man with sad eyes, and all her life Mom had been a pushover for sad eyes. Poor Papa's photograph is proof of this. And so, two minutes after Inspector Millner stepped into the apartment, Mom's expression softened. There was almost a smile underneath her frown. Her handshake was definitely gracious. She spoke as sharp as ever to me, and as poisonously sweet as ever to Shirley, but when she turned to Inspector Millner she suddenly became the perfect hostess, full of consideration for her guest's comfort and full of interest in his conversation.

During dinner the evening reached its high point. The talk, drifted, naturally, to homicide. Mom asked me what was the latest case I was working on, and she was delighted to hear that Inspector Millner and I were currently working on the same case. "It's a good thing for my crazy son," she said, "the influence of a sensible older man."

But Inspector Millner didn't look delighted at all. "The things that people will do to each other," he said. "To their fellow human beings. Thirty-two years on the force, and it still amazes me."

Mom laughed. "Fifty-two years in the Bronx, and nothing amazes me!"

"Terrible, terrible," said Inspector Millner. "That any man— You tell her about it, Dave. It burns me up just to think of it—I'll get all mixed up."

MOM IN THE SPRING

I saw Mom turn a quick look of sympathy on Inspector Millner —at which Shirley and I exchanged significant glances. Then I started in.

"The thing that makes us feel especially bad," I said, "is that we were warned about this crime ahead of time. About a week ago this couple came to us—Edward Winters and his wife Edith. Man in his late thirties, thin and pasty-faced, horn-rimmed glasses, weak and sort of fussy manner. Woman a little younger, small but very cool and calm and dominating. Obviously has her husband completely under her thumb. The sort of relationship that makes a man cynical about marriage—"

I caught a look from Shirley at this. So I added hastily, "That is, some marriages. Mostly, of course, marriage is the most wonderful institution in life, and nobody should be without it."

"So go on with the story," Mom said, and there was a little glitter in her eye which pulled me up short for a moment. Was it possible, I wondered, that she had some inkling of what Shirley and I were up to? But that's silly, I told myself; she couldn't suspect a thing.

"This Mr. and Mrs. Winters," I went on, "were worried about their Old Aunt Margaret. Old Aunt Margaret, they explained, was in her late fifties. She was a small, delicate, slightly faded lady who had never got married. She lived by herself in an old two-story private house just off Fifth Avenue, and her only family in the world was her nephew Edward and his wife Edith. She was devoted to them, they said, and they were devoted to her. They had dinner with the old lady two or three times every week. She took them with her to the theater. They chose her clothes for her, and remembered her birthday, and generally made her life worth living. That's their story, anyway."

"You're leaving out the money," Mom said.

I looked up at Mom, astonished. And I saw that Inspector Millner was looking astonished, too.

"The fact that this nice delicate Aunt Margaret had a lot of money," Mom said. "And her nephew and his wife don't have so much money. This fact you left out."

"Mom, how did you guess that?" I said.

MY MOTHER, THE DETECTIVE

"Guess? Who guesses?" Mom glared at me. "You told this to me. In between the lines you told me. A woman lives in a two-story private house off Fifth Avenue—this is a woman with money. When it comes to rents and taxes, Fifth Avenue isn't the Bronx."

"But the nephew and his wife," said Inspector Millner. "How did you know that they *don't* have any money?"

"What Davie said—'she took them with her to the theater.' The usual procedure is, loving nephews and their wives are the ones who take the poor old aunt to the theater. This way it's pretty certain Aunt Margaret was buying the tickets."

"Smart," said Inspector Millner, bobbing his head. "Practically professional."

"She was buying the tickets, all right," I said. "In fact, the Winters pair weren't in the office five minutes before I had them pegged—they were sponging off their aunt. Winters doesn't seem to do anything in particular by way of making a living. He calls himself an architect, but he admits that he hasn't built any houses lately. He devotes his time to working on this complicated plan of his for tearing down and rebuilding New York City. His wife doesn't have any money of her own—she's a girl from the Midwest who worked as a secretary before she got married. And yet, they're well-dressed, they've got a nice apartment in the East Sixties, and they don't show signs of stinting themselves on anything. Where does the money come from? There's no other place but Aunt Margaret.

"So, anyway, they came to Homicide all upset over Aunt Margaret. They were positive that somebody was out to kill her. In fact, they could even tell us this somebody's name. A tobacco planter from Louisville, Kentucky, named Thomas Keith."

"Just a minute," said Shirley, who occasionally likes to show Mom that she can do the detecting trick herself. "There's a discrepancy in what you said. If Aunt Margaret was all alone in the world—a timid old maid whose life revolved around her nephew and his wife—how on earth did she ever meet this Kentucky tobacco planter?"

"Now that's a simple question," said Mom, who likes to show Shirley that the detecting trick isn't as easy as some people think. "An old maid who lives alone, with nobody in her life except a couple of

50

schnorrer relatives—this smells of only one thing. Letters to the personal columns. Lonely Hearts advertisements. There's a certain type nice, weak-minded woman that always breaks out eventually in letters."

"Amazing!" said the Inspector.

"That's just what happened, Mom," I said. "A few months ago the Winters couple went to visit Aunt Margaret in her house. While she was out of the room they happened to notice this letter lying on the floor where it had dropped accidentally. It was a letter from this Thomas Keith. They confronted Aunt Margaret with it, and she confessed the whole thing. She had put her name in the personal column of some magazine—one of those messages about a 'refined intelligent lady anxious to correspond with a cultured, middle-aged, gentleman.' And so on—you know the type. This Keith answered her ad. By the time she told her nephew and his wife about these letters, she and Keith had become very chummy indeed. He was writing her what a deep influence she had on his life, and she was glowing and sparkling like a young girl at her first dance."

"And those no-good relatives of hers didn't like this?" said Mom, looking particularly sour. "They don't think a woman over fifty is entitled to any joy in her life?"

Shirley and I couldn't help exchanging glances at this—glances of triumph almost, premature as they might have been.

"They certainly didn't like it," I went on. "Right away they started to put the pressure on Aunt Margaret. They told her it was silly, it was childish, it was dangerous; that he was only after her money, he was making a fool of her, he might be planning to do her some harm. But the more they worked on her, the more she hardened against them. Ordinarily she was an unaggressive, easily dominated lady, but her relationship with this Keith, even though she hadn't ever set eyes on him, seemed to be terribly important to her. She told her nephew and his wife that she wouldn't stop writing to Keith, no matter what. This was the first real friendship she'd ever had in her life. *They* had friends of their own, so why shouldn't *she*?"

"Good for Aunt Margaret," said Mom, nodding vigorously.

MY MOTHER, THE DETECTIVE

"Good for Aunt Margaret," said Inspector Millner, like a small echo.

"What's more," I went on, "the opposition of her nephew and his wife made Aunt Margaret write even warmer and friendlier letters to Keith than ever. And pretty soon a hint of matrimony began to show itself between the lines. Edward and Edith Winters were in a fury. There must've been some pretty heated scenes with their aunt. They claim they didn't raise their voices to her—but that Edith Winters looks like she could do more damage with one quiet word than most people can do with a whole bombardment of shouts. Finally, after one particularly sentimental letter from Keith, the Winters couple came to us.

"They wanted us to put Keith in jail. Men like that are menaces, they said. Swindlers, confidence men, and even worse—potential murderers. It seems that Edward Winters's own mother, who passed away a while back, was victimized by one of these Lonely Hearts ads about twenty-five years ago. Some swindler took her for a lot of money and she never got over the disillusionment. All in all, this has made her son especially bitter on the subject. But if you ask me, his bitterness also had a little bit to do with his reluctance to share Aunt Margaret's fortune with some Kentucky tobacco planter.

"Well, we had to tell Winters and his wife that we couldn't help them. Keith lived in a different state—no crime had been committed—and Aunt Margaret had a perfect right to correspond with anybody she pleased. Edith Winters got very annoyed at this. She and her husband had sneaked one of Keith's letters out of Aunt Margaret's desk, and she pulled it out now just to prove to us what a phony he was. It was pretty phony-sounding, all right—but there still wasn't anything we could do."

"How was it phony?" Mom said. "Give me a for instance."

I thought that over a minute. "Well—it was full of high-flown flattery and super-southern expressions, like 'my little magnolia blossom' and 'star of my life' and so on. It was written in a kind of small, spidery hand, with the letters all fancy and full of curleycues—you know that old-fashioned style of penmanship.

MOM IN THE SPRING

"But the worst part of the letter was in the P.S. For a minute he dropped the 'heart's delight' and 'my own little angel' line and mentioned specifically how he was looking forward to actually meeting her face to face in the near future. 'The last time I visited your great city,' he wrote, 'was in the year 1929, and I was alone and my heart was empty. I saw the Statue of Liberty and to me it was only hollow stone. I looked down from the top of your Empire State Building, and spread below me were only rooftops and smokestacks. I strolled through your Central Park, and the trees spoke not a word to me. But soon I will come again, and my heart will be full, and you will be on my arm, and New York will become a city of magic.' Honest to God, Mom, that's exactly what this man wrote. And poor Aunt Margaret fell for it hook, line, and sinker."

Mom shrugged. "This is typical man's reasoning. The men give out the fancy flattery, the men go wild from disappointment if the women don't fall for this fancy flattery—and as soon as the women do fall, the men start sneering and saying, 'Those dumb women!' "

"All men aren't like that," Shirley felt she had to put in. "Some men have the greatest respect and admiration for women."

Mom gave Shirley a smile—another of those quick smiles that made me wonder just how much she suspected. But my wondering didn't last long, because Mom was pressing me to go on with the story.

"Well, Mr. and Mrs. Winters stormed out of the office," I said. "If we wouldn't help them, they said, they'd do something about the situation themselves. We found out later what they did. Edward Winters took the plane that night to Louisville, to talk to this Thomas Keith and warn him off. He couldn't find Keith's number in the phone book, though—you'll find out why in a minute. So Winters flew back to New York in the morning. And when he saw his aunt that afternoon, she was terribly excited. She had received a telegram from Keith. It came collect—collect, mind you! Can you imagine the nerve of the man? He wired that he was coming to New York that same night 'to claim his dearest heart's delight forever.'

"Well, the old lady was in quite a state over this. Evidently she never expected her friendship to go quite so far. Now that it had come to the point of actually marrying the man, she seemed to lose her nerve. She was scared and upset. She pleaded with her nephew and his wife to have dinner with her that night, and to stay with her in the house till Keith arrived. They waited till after midnight—so the Winters couple tell us—but Keith didn't show up. Finally, the Winters couple left.

"In the morning they called up Aunt Margaret. No answer on the phone. So they went over to her house, found the front door unlocked, and discovered her body on the living-room floor. She had been strangled to death with one of her own scarves. Keith's telegram was clutched in her right hand. It was pretty clear what had happened. Her Southern Romeo had showed up after the nephew and his wife left. He told her that he had come to marry her. She told him that she had changed her mind and didn't want to marry him—remember how upset she was at receiving his telegram? So he killed her in a fit of anger—and maybe hoping to find some money in the apartment. And there you are—that's our case."

We were all silent for a while, eating our pot-roast. Finally Mom gave a nod of her head, "So what are you up to now?" she said. "Have you got the police from Kentucky running all over the place, looking for this Thomas Keith?"

"That's all over with," I said. "We extradited Keith yesterday, and we've got him in jail right now."

"He's an animal," said Inspector Millner. "Some people just aren't human."

But Mom was staring at me hard. "You mean you actually found him? There was actually a fellow by that name?"

"Oh, I see what you mean, Mom," I said with a laugh. "Naturally Keith was a phony name—he used it just to sign those letters to Aunt Margaret. But we located him easy enough by his photograph."

"Photograph!" Mom sat up straight and gave me her most exasperated look. "Now why are you hiding the important facts, if you please? Do you think maybe it would be too easy for me if you told me everything? Where, if I may ask, did you find this photograph?"

"In the old lady's bedroom. Underneath her pillow, to be exact. She actually slept with this man's photograph under her pillow. We checked with the files, and sure enough it was the photograph of an old-time confidence man named Sam Kidd—same thick black mustache, same highly polished hair. Used to be active all over the East. He was arrested in New York in 1929, and served fifteen years in prison down South. After he got out, he presumably went straight. The authorities kept their eye on him, of course. They told us he was in the haberdashery business and had never gone up north again. But of course, he must've been working this Lonely Hearts racket on the side."

"That's the type swindler he was back in 1929?" Mom said. "The Lonely Hearts type?"

"Among other types," I said. "He's built for it, Mom. You should see him. He's older than our official photograph shows, of course—nowadays the mustache is gray and the hair is white. But he's still as oily and smooth as ever. Not hard to understand why a lonely old lady would fall for him."

"It shows how dangerous it is to be lonely old lady," Shirley put in.

"That's a fact," said Mom. "People are always trying to make matches for you, and other such dangers."

While Shirley fidgeted, Mom turned back to me. "And you found this fellow living in Kentucky? Right there in Looie's Ville?"

"No, not in Louisville. I admit that's one of the weaknesses in our case. This Sam Kidd's been running a haberdashery store in Atlanta, Georgia. He claims he's never been to Louisville in his life. He says he never heard of Aunt Margaret or her family. And unfortunately the girl in the Louisville telegraph office didn't particularly notice the man who sent that wire to Aunt Margaret. Also unfortunately, the handwriting experts won't say definitely that the letters are in his handwriting. To them it looks like a disguised handwriting. On the other hand, we got one break—Kidd has no alibi for the night of the murder. He could very easily have flown to New York, killed Aunt Margaret, then flown right back to Atlanta again."

MY MOTHER, THE DETECTIVE

"It's a good case," said Inspector Millner. "God knows I wouldn't want to see a man punished for something he didn't do. But this dirty dog—that poor harmless lady—it's definitely a good case."

"It's a wonderful case," Mom said. "The only trouble with it is, it don't have much connection with the truth."

By this time in my life I am used to these sudden, upsetting pronouncements from Mom. I take them in my stride. I shrug or I smile in a superior way. Deep down I may be groaning to myself. I may be telling myself, "Not again—she isn't going to do this to me again!" But this is deep down. On the surface I remain cool and unperturbed.

Poor Inspector Millner, though, was having his first experience with Mom's pronouncements. Cool and unperturbed were definitely not the words for him at that moment. "But I don't understand," he said. "How can you say—I mean, what makes you—I mean, you seem so sure of yourself—"

"Sure? Who's sure?" Mom said. "I got my ideas. But first I'm interested in the answer to four small questions. After that I'll be sure."

Inspector Millner looked even more confused. "Four questions? I don't follow. What four questions?"

I hurried to his rescue. "It's nothing. Mom likes to ask questions. She takes an interest in these things. Just sort of polite curiosity—" But really I was terribly anxious. Mom's "small questions" have a way of getting wild and woolly sometimes—and I didn't want Inspector Millner to get the idea that she was out of her head, "Go ahead, Mom," I said, my heart sinking. "Ask your questions."

She turned to me, very businesslike. "Question One. These letters that Aunt Margaret got from this Thomas Keith what was the postmark on them? Did they definitely come from Looie's Ville?"

The question wasn't wild at all—it actually made sense. I breathed a sigh of relief, and I noticed Shirley doing likewise. "I see what you're getting at, Mom" I said. "Suppose Sam Kidd didn't mail those letters from Louisville at all. Suppose he mailed them right from Atlanta. The postmarks would show that, and we'd have very strong evidence against him. I'm afraid it's a blind valley, though.

Aunt Margaret didn't save the envelopes of those letters. The Winters couple told us that she threw all away."

"Good," Mom said. "I'm glad to hear it."

"Glad to hear it? But Mom, that's not good news at all—"

But Mom was pushing on. "Question Two. Aunt Margaret was like a lot of old maids, wasn't she, very neat and tidy? She kept her place and herself clean like a new pin, didn't she?"

This made me a little uneasy again. Because this second question didn't make quite as much sense as the first. Fortunately, though, Mom was right. "Yes, she was the neat, orderly type," I said. "We could tell that when we searched her house."

"Question Three," Mom said. "Is it possible that this no-good nephew, aside from the fact that he's always been living off his aunt's money, is also a big tightwad? He's the stingy type, am I right?"

My uneasiness grew. I laughed, trying to pass off Mom's question as a joke. "Well, I don't see what bearing that has—"

"You don't have to see. Only answer."

"Well—it's actually a coincidence that you asked that question. We talked to the servants, neighbors, local tradesmen, and so on— the people who came in contact with Winters and his wife. They *did* say that he is well-known in the neighborhood for his stinginess. Willing enough to spend money on his own comfort, you understand, but small and mean in his dealings with other people." Even as I said this, I could see the bewildered look on Inspector Millner's face. "What's your last question, Mom," I said, putting a slight emphasis on the word "last."

"Question Four and Last," Mom said. "In these letters that Aunt Margaret got from Thomas Keith there a lot of words underlined?"

"Underlined!" In spite of my concern over Inspector Millner, I couldn't help gaping at this. "Underlined—now how the—"

"Underlined," Mom said impatiently. "With lines under them. All of a sudden my English is no good?"

"Yes, there was lots of underlining," I said. "All through those letters. But Mom, I just don't understand—"

Inspector Millner leaned forward and spoke to Mom in a slow earnest voice, the way you speak to sick people or to children. "Do you think it's some sort of code?" he said. "I mean, foreign agents or something, and they underline the key words?"

"Code?" Mom turned a look of wry amusement on him. "I suppose you could call it this. To some people it might be a code."

This remark was so completely inexplicable that the rest of us could do nothing but fidget and look embarrassed. Finally Shirley broke the silence. "Now what, Mother? Now that you've asked your questions, are you willing to admit that the police have the right man?"

"The right man!" Mom gave a snort. "The right man is walking around free right now."

It was one of Mom's usual bombshells. And we all reacted appropriately. Inspector Millner was especially bewildered. "But what have you found out? We didn't tell you anything that we didn't know already. I really don't mean to contradict—"

"I didn't find out anything that you didn't know already," Mom said. "But I found it out with my head, not with my flat feet." An instant later she turned an apologetic smile on Inspector Millner. "I'm not referring to your flat feet, naturally. Only the younger men—" Her apologetic smile turned into a sharp look, directed at me.

"All right, Mom," I said, with a long sigh—because I was convinced that her chances with Inspector Millner were completely ruined by this time. I was sure she had scared off the poor man forever. "Let's hear it and get it over with. What's the solution to the murder? Where did the stupid police go wrong?"

"You went wrong," Mom said, "by forgetting the most important factor—Mr. Feinberg, the butcher."

Inspector Millner blinked. "But please," he said in a feeble voice. "Who's Mr. Feinberg, the butcher? He hasn't even appeared in the case up till now—"

"What about Feinberg, the butcher?" I said to Mom, very quietly.

"I'm explaining," Mom said. "During the last war, do you remember the meat shortage? Poor Feinberg the butcher, for a long time he didn't have no chopped hamburger to sell to his customers.

MOM IN THE SPRING

What complaining we heard from him! One day some woman comes into the store and tells him an interesting story she just read in a history book—how the French butchers in the days of Napoleon's Boneypart, when there was also a meat shortage, used to kill the cats and serve them up for hamburger. Feinberg listened very thoughtful to this story. And the next morning, when we came in to buy our meat, what a surprise, he had a whole new supply of hamburger for us! And also what a surprise, the two cats that usually crawled around his store weren't crawling around no more! Believe me, there wasn't many of us buying Feinberg's hamburger that morning. Like we said to each other, 'Coincidences is very nice, but some of them are maybe a little too convenient for a good digestion.' "

"And this long and elaborate story," Shirley said, "is supposed to have some connection with this murder?"

"I think I see it," said Inspector Millner hesitantly. "Feinberg the butcher is really—"

Mom nodded with tremendous approval. "A smart policeman," she said. "Who would believe it? I finally met a smart policeman. So now it's as plain as my nose, isn't it? For instance, take the telegram that Aunt Margaret got from this Keith in Louie's Ville. A collect telegram, didn't you tell me? Here is this swindler who wants to marry an old maid for her money. It's part of his plan to make her believe he's a big tobacco planter with plenty money of his own. Until he's finally got her sewed up in the license, can he afford to drop this act? No, he can't. So is he going to be fool enough to send her a *collect* telegram?"

"Of course he isn't!" Inspector Millner cried. "Why didn't I see that right away?"

"At least you're a big enough man to admit it," Mom said. "But this isn't the only evidence. Take the photograph, for instance. You find it under Aunt Margaret's pillow. It's a photograph of this Keith which he's supposed to have sent her in one of his letters. But here's the important fact—it's a photograph which was taken twenty-five years ago, before he went to jail in 1929. Same black hair, same black mustache—didn't you say so yourself? And today he's a man with white hair and a gray mustache. Now a swindler who's planning

59

to show up in person and marry a rich old maid, does he send her a twenty-five-year-old photograph? What happens when she finally meets him and sees what he really looks like? Big disappointment. Maybe the whole wedding falls through. Excuse me, he don't take such a chance. So the answer is, he never sent her this photograph at all."

"All right, Mom," I said. "This seems to prove that Sam Kidd didn't——"

"More evidence," Mom said, ignoring me. "We proved that Sammy Kidd didn't send that telegram from Louie's Ville. We also proved that he didn't send his photograph to Aunt Margaret. Now we'll prove that he didn't write any of those letters at all."

"Yes, of course he didn't," Inspector Millner broke in, quite excited. "It's been bothering me all along, but I couldn't put my finger on it. The Empire State Building——"

"Aha!" said Mom, raising her finger. "I was waiting if somebody would catch the Empire State Building."

I was more confused than ever. "What about it, Mom?"

"In that letter you read us," Mom said, "that letter from this Keith, you remember how he talks about going up to the top of the Empire State Building and looking down at the rooftops?"

"But that's a normal thing, Mom. People do it every day."

"Exactly. People do it every day—nowadays. A person who lives in New York, and who always lived in New York, such a person thinks of this as a normal thing. Us New Yorkers, we take it for granted, the Empire State Building. If we wanted to make up a phony-baloney story about a Southerner remembering his last trip to New York, naturally we'd put in the Empire State Building. What we don't think of is, the Empire State Building wasn't with us since the beginning of the world."

"1931," Inspector Millner put in.

"The Empire State Building wasn't finished till 1931. And Keith, in his letter, says that his last visit to New York was in 1929."

"So there it is, in words from one syllable," Mom said. "This Sammy Kidd, he really was in New York for the last time in 1929. Since then he's been in jail and down in Atlanta, Georgia. So why would he have to tell a lie about visiting the Empire State Building on his last trip to New York? He could just as easy tell the honest truth about that trip. But this letter was written by somebody who lived in New York right through till today, and who forgot when the Empire State Building was finished."

"But Mom," I cried, unable to stand it any longer. "You've proved that Sam Kidd didn't write those letters—and that means that he wasn't the one who killed the old lady. But who *did* write the letters? Who *did* kill her?"

"Feinberg, the butcher!" Inspector Millner put in triumphantly.

I stared at him, half astounded, half delighted. My God, he was beginning to talk and think like Mom already!

"Feinberg, the butcher, is right," Mom nodding her head approvingly. "Who was it that did live in New York City right through till now? Who was it that could get his hands easily on a twenty-five-year-old photograph of a Lonely Hearts swindler—because his own mother was writing to such a swindler twenty-five years ago? And it was this old photograph which he dug up out of the attic or the basement and planted under the old lady's pillow for the purpose of fooling the police—"

"I see it, I see it," I said.

"—and who was it," Mom went on, "that we know was definitely in Louie's Ville, by his own confession, at the time this telegram was sent to Aunt Margaret? And the biggest evidence yet, who is it that would be most likely to send this telegram collect? Who was a well-known tightwad? Who was small and mean in his dealings—according to your own words, Davie? Who had such a bad stinginess, and such a strong habit of sponging from Aunt Margaret, that he couldn't resist the temptation to send a collect telegram?"

"It's the nephew, Mom," I cried out. "He invented this mythical Thomas Keith himself. He answered Aunt Margaret's ad in the personal column. He wrote all those letters. He went down to Louisville—not to talk to Keith as he claimed, but simply to send the telegram Then he killed Aunt Margaret that night, put the photograph under her pillow, and 'discovered' the body next morning. A pretty ingenious frame-up—he not only pins his crime on a scape-goat, he actually creates that scapegoat right out of his own head."

But Inspector Millner was frowning and shaking his head. "But that's not the whole story. It wasn't the nephew alone. There's the evidence of the handwriting."

Mom was so pleased with him that she laughed out loud. "Good for you. The handwriting, naturally. Small and spidery, you said, Davie—like an old man. But small and spidery is also like a woman's handwriting. And the letters were fancy and curleycued. Definitely something a woman would do. And a lot of the words were under-lined—a typical woman's trick. Didn't I read it in a history novel once, how one of those Queens from England—Queen Victorious, wasn't it?—had the habit from underlining the words in her letters?"

"The nephew's wife, of course," I said. "I should've seen that all along. She's the strong-minded one—her husband's strictly a mouse. *She* wrote those letters. She thought up the whole scheme. I'll bet she was even the one who did the actual—" This thought made me shudder a little, and I broke off.

"Feinberg, the butcher, all over again," Mom said, with satis-faction. "For years and years the nephew and his wife are living off their aunt. For years and years they keep her cut off so she's got nobody else in the world to give her money to. All of a sudden somebody else comes into her life, it looks like she might even get married to this somebody else, and her money isn't so safe for this nephew and his wife no more. So all of a sudden Aunt Margaret gets killed—and what a surprise, the nephew and his wife, being her only relatives, have got their hands on her money for good! Believe me, Davie, this is a load of chopped hamburger that positively has a cat in it. And this cat, I think, is big enough even for the New York City Homicide Squad."

Inspector Millner started to his feet. "I think maybe I'd better call homicide. We can't let that pair run loose—"

"Just a minute!"

This time it was Shirley who spoke up. There was a sharpness in her voice which made Inspector Millner take his seat again, and which made the rest of us turn and look at her.

MOM IN THE SPRING

"One thing isn't clear yet," Shirley said. "When old Aunt Margaret received those letters from Thomas Keith, they must've had Louisville postmarks on them. A New York City postmark would have aroused her suspicions. So how did Edward and Edith Winters arrange to send those letters from Louisville?"

"Yes, how about that, Mom?" I said. And we all turned to Mom and waited for her answer.

A strange thing happened. Instead of settling this question with a few masterful words, Mom suddenly grew very uneasy. A touch of red came to her cheeks. She lowered her eyes and mumbled, "Time for dessert, everybody pass in their plates, please."

"No you don't, Mother," said Shirley, a gleam of triumph in her eye. "Answer my question."

Mom hesitated a moment, then she looked up at us. And the expression on her face gave me a start. It was so sad—so sad and miserable. "Mom, what is it?" I said. "Are you sick or something?"

Mom shook her head, and gave a sigh. "I didn't want to say it," she said. "It started off as a secret, it should stay a secret. If you want I should tell you about it, then you got to make me a promise. Every one of you, you got to promise—outside of this room tonight, it'll still be a secret."

One by one, puzzled as we were, we made that promise.

Mom gave another sigh, and then she started speaking. "It's just like my cousin Hannah's grandnephew, little Joel," she said. "Poor little boy. He was naturally shy from the start. His Mama and Papa were such big butterflies, lots of parties, but no attention for little Joel. And his big thick glasses didn't make it no easier for him. He didn't have no friends, this is the point of the story. It was a terrible shame to him. He got the idea that people was laughing at him because he was such a *schlemiel* he couldn't even find friends for himself. So what did he do, that boy? It was only human, wasn't it? He made up friends. He made up their names, their looks, their families. He told stories about the games he played with them. Such careful, realistic stories. For the benefit of other people, of course—and a little bit for the benefit of himself." Mom paused for a moment, then she finished up. "Old ladies and little children—there isn't so much difference between them."

We all stared at her. "Mom," I said, "do you mean—"

"By yourself you should've guessed it," Mom said. "The handwriting on that letter. Certainly it was a woman's handwriting. But that fancy curleycue business—this isn't the habit of a young modern woman, this is the habit of an old-fashioned woman. This is how we used to do it when I was a little girl. And the underlining, the way so many words was underlined. This isn't the type thing that a cold, unemotional woman like this Winters woman goes in for. This is the habit of a lonely, excitable woman with lots of feelings and sentimentality."

"*She wrote them to herself,*" said Inspector Millner, his voice trembling a little. "She was lonely, and her nephew and his wife were always reminding her of her loneliness. So she decided to show them that she could have a real friendship of her own."

"And that's why she never showed them the envelopes," I said. "Those letters never *had* any envelopes."

"Exactly," said Mom. "And this is also why the nephew and his wife found that letter 'accidentally' on the floor. A neat, tidy lady like that Aunt Margaret, she don't leave important letters accidentally on the floor when company's coming. She *wanted* them to find the letter and know about her friend Keith—this was the most important part of her plan. Just like little Joel."

"But Mom," I said, thoughtfully. "She had her nephew and his wife completely fooled, didn't she? They didn't have any idea that she was writing those letters to herself, did they? They believed that there really was a man in Louisville, didn't they? So weren't they taking a big chance, planting that photograph and trying to pin the crime on that man? Now could they feel sure that he wouldn't get in touch with the police, and prove that the man in the photograph wasn't him?"

"Sure they couldn't be," Mom said. "But they could be *pretty* sure. All the chances was that this fellow in Louie's Ville, when he heard about the murder, would keep as far away from the police as he could. Especially since the police had a photograph of somebody else—so why should he stick his neck out? But all right, even if he *did* stick his neck, even if he went to the police and said, 'I'm the fellow that was writing to this old lady, and that isn't my photograph you found under her pillow'—all right, it still looks suspicious for him. A confidence man who's trying to get his hands on all old lady's money, it's just possible, even if he never intended to meet the old lady personally, that he might send her *somebody else's* picture. Either way —you follow me?—it would look bad for the man from Louie's Ville, but it wouldn't look bad at all for the nephew and his wife."

We all thought this over for a moment—and then, suddenly, a look of horror came over Inspector Millner's face. "The telegram!" he cried. "We've—that is, you've—already proved that the telegram was sent to her by her own nephew. That poor lady—imagine what she felt when she got that telegram? A telegram *from a man that she knew didn't exist*! No wonder she was so frightened and upset."

I took it up from there. "She didn't know what was happening. It was just as if her daydream had suddenly come to life before her eyes. And she was ashamed to tell the truth to her nephew and his wife."

"If only she had, if only she had," said Inspector Millner, shaking his head back and forth. "They wouldn't have done it then. They wouldn't have had any reason to do it."

"If only she had," said Mom. Her voice was soft and gentle—I hadn't heard such gentleness in her voice since I was a little boy, since I had pneumonia and Mom sat up with me all night during the crisis. "A little bit of love that was strictly her own," Mom said. "This is all she wanted in the world. And even this she couldn't have without giving up her life for it." Mom's eyes were on me, and her smile was tender. "Some people in this world just don't have the luck," she said.

For a long time we were all silent.

The dessert, one of Mom's nesselrode pies, was waiting unnoticed. We were embarrassed and uneasy as if old Aunt Margaret had been right at the table with us, blushing

A moment later the mood broke. Mom lifted her chin and laughed and said, "All right, the last five minutes didn't happen.

We're back to the dessert. Kindly pass your plates, please." We passed our plates, Inspector Millner phoned Homicide, and Shirley started talking about the new spring hats. Then Mom told a joke—about her next-door neighbor, Mrs. Korngold, and the dinner ended in noise and laughter.

When they said goodbye that night, Mom and Inspector Millner shook hands for an unusually long time—Shirley and I were timing it. And when Mom said, "Come again—come again soon," I knew this wasn't mere politeness. Mom isn't the sort of person who goes in for mere politeness. And all the way down in the elevator, Inspector Millner kept shaking his head and saying, "A wonderful woman."

The next morning I called Mom up and fished casually for information.

"He's a swell guy, isn't he?" I said. "Inspector Millner, I mean."

"Herbie, you mean?" Mom said. "He's a nice man. He needs a little fattening up, though. A few good dinners would do it."

Shirley and I spent the rest of the morning congratulating ourselves—and planning the next steps in the campaign. As I mentioned already, it was really a beautiful spring.

MOM SHEDS A TEAR

"THE PITTER-PUTTER OF LITTLE FEET," MOM said, managing to sigh sentimentally and point her finger at me accusingly, both at the same time. "It's one of the chief pleasures in life. I don't know what's the matter with you and Shirley, that you're not interested in this pleasure."

I smiled a little sheepishly, as I always do when Mom, in her sharp disconcerting way, brings up this subject. "Shirley and I are very anxious to have kids," I said. "As soon as I get my raise, and we can afford the down payment on a house in the suburbs—"

"Down payments! Raises!" Mom gave an angry toss of her head. "Young people nowadays, sometimes I think they got checkbooks where their feelings should be. Believe me, Davie, if your Papa and me worried our heads over down payments when we was your age, believe me you wouldn't be sitting here eating this pot-roast right now."

It was Friday night. The next day was my day off from the Homicide Squad, so of course I was having my weekly dinner up in the Bronx with Mom. My wife Shirley wasn't with me tonight, though. She was out in Chicago for a week, visiting her folks. And as usual, Mom felt that Shirley's absence entitled her to get terribly personal—downright embarrassing, in fact—about my married life.

"Besides, Mom," I said, trying to turn the conversation into a joke, "aren't you the one who's always telling me that children are more trouble than they're worth? You know your favorite saying— 'They break your furniture when they're babies, and they break your heart when they grow up.' "

"Who's denying it?" Mom snapped back at me. "And without such heartbreaks what would life be?"

"I wonder if you'd feel like that," I said, "if you were Agnes Fisher."

67

MY MOTHER, THE DETECTIVE

"Agnes Fisher? I don't know her. There's a Sadie Fishbaum on the third floor—"

"Agnes Fisher is involved in a case I started on yesterday. She's a widow, and she has a little boy five years old named Kenneth."

"And what's the matter with him, this little Kenny Fisher?"

"Nothing that we'll ever be able to prove. But all the indications are that little five-year-old Kenneth Fisher is a murderer."

Mom lowered her fork and glared at me. For a long time she glared, so hard that I had to turn my eyes away guiltily, even though I had no idea what I was feeling guilty about. Finally she gave a long sarcastic sigh: "It's finally happened. Haven't I been predicting it for years? Associating all the time with dope fiends and homopathic maniacs and drunk drivers, it finally went to your head. It only goes to show, when you had a chance to go into the shirt business with your Uncle Simon, why didn't you listen to your mother?"

"Take it easy, Mom. I'm not the one who's crazy. It's this Fisher case. I'll tell you about it, and you can judge for yourself."

Obviously unconvinced, Mom brought her fork to her lips again, took a ladylike mouthful, and settled down to hear my story.

"Agnes Fisher is in her early thirties," I said, "very pretty and breathless and a little absent-minded—in a nice attractive way, you understand. Her husband died a year ago—he was an Air Force pilot in Korea and she lives with her little boy Kenneth in the house that her husband left her. It's a four-story house on Washington Square, one of the few old-time red-brick houses of that type that's left on the Square. It's been in the Fisher family since the nineteenth century."

"He had money, this Mr. Fisher?" Mom said.

"The Fishers are a wealthy old New York family. Not so wealthy as they used to be, I guess, but still doing pretty well. So anyway, Agnes Fisher lived on Washington Square quite peacefully, getting along nicely with her friends and neighbors, apparently reconciling herself to her widowhood. But her little boy's life wasn't quite so calm and happy. The death of his father evidently upset him badly. He's a naturally shy, dreamy kid, and with his father gone he sort of went into his shell more than ever. He spent lots of time by himself. He seemed to prefer his own day dreams to the company of other kids. And then, a few months ago, somebody new came into the lives of the boy and his mother.

"The newcomer was Nelson Fisher, little Kenneth's uncle, his father's younger brother. Nelson Fisher was about thirty years old. Like his late brother he was an Air Force pilot. He had just been discharged from the service, not because he wanted to be—flying was his whole life—but because he had contracted malaria in the Pacific. He needed care and attention, and his sister-in-law Agnes is his only responsible relative. She's a kind-hearted woman, and she was happy to take him in. She gave him the whole third floor of the old house, and so he moved in with his sister-in-law and his little nephew."

"And little Kenny was jealous maybe?" Mom said.

"At first he was jealous. He sulked in a corner, or he cried and carried on, or he looked daggers at his uncle. Nelson Fisher was still a sick man—he still had after-effects from his malaria, and what with his medicines, his dizzy spells, his chills, his weekly visits from the doctor, Agnes did a lot of fussing over him. Kenneth seemed to resent this. One day he even went into a tantrum over it. He jumped up and down and yelled hysterically, "*He's* not my father! I don't want *him* for my father!" He finally calmed down, but the incident upset his mother terribly. And it caused a lot of talk among the servants."

"This was only at first though?" Mom said. "Afterwards little Kenny changed his opinion of his uncle?"

"His antagonism lasted about a month. Then, all of a sudden, he developed a completely different attitude. One day he couldn't stand the sight of Nelson, the next day he couldn't stand to be *out* of Nelson's sight. Suddenly he had a case of genuine, full-fledged hero-worship. He dogged his poor uncle's heels. He trotted after him wherever he went. He bombarded him with questions, and whatever answers he got he believed them implicitly. He gaped in admiration at everything his Uncle Nelson did or said."

"So this is normal enough in little children," Mom said. "They change their minds for no logical reason. And incidentally, I've also known some grown-ups—"

MY MOTHER, THE DETECTIVE

"Oh, it was normal all right," I said. "Anyway, it seemed to be. It's only because of what happened later— But I won't get ahead of my story. For a few months everything was fine in the Fisher home. Nelson seemed to enjoy his nephew's company. He had never married and had any kids of his own, and he treated Kenneth like a younger brother. Very ideal relationship. And then, about week ago, at the beginning of the summer, little Kenneth started to do peculiar things. Until a week ago, he had always been a fairly honest kid. And then, a week ago, he started to steal things."

"Steal things?" said Mom, poking her head forward. "So what did he steal?"

"Always the same kind of thing, Mom. Things that belonged to his dead father. For instance, it started with Agnes noticing that her husband's medal, a Silver Star, was missing. She kept it in the jewelry case in her dresser drawer, along with cufflinks, wedding ring, and other things, but now it was gone. She sounded out the cook and the housemaid as indirectly as she could, but they both got very indignant and insisted that they weren't thieves. For a while she suspected that the man who had come to fix the plumbing was the guilty one. And then, the next morning, the housemaid came to her very triumphantly, holding up the medal. She had found it, she said, while she was making up Kenneth's bed just a few minutes before. The medal was under Kenneth's pillow. Agnes was puzzled. She asked Kenneth about it but he wouldn't give her any explanation. He just turned his eyes away, mumbled something, then ran off. And Agnes isn't the strong-willed, domineering type of mother who could keep pounding at the boy until she got the truth out of him.

"And then Kenneth did it again. In one of the hall closets Agnes keeps a lot of miscellaneous things stored in boxes—some of her husband's old clothes, his books and papers, and so on. One day she was passing this closet when she heard a rattling inside. She opened the door and saw Kenneth. He had pulled down one of the boxes, torn it open, and was about to take away something from inside of it.

"Believe it or not, Mom, Kenneth was stealing one of those long, flowing old-fashioned opera capes that people used to wear fifty years ago. It had belonged to Kenneth's father. When he was an undergraduate at Princeton, he had appeared in a sort of Gay Nineties revue presented by the dramatic society. This old opera cape was part of his costume for that show."

"And little Kenny knew, definitely knew, that his Papa wore this opera cape once?"

"He couldn't help but know, Mom. There's a photograph of his father in the living room of the house taken after the performance of the revue and showing him with the opera cape over his shoulders. Well, Agnes naturally made Kenneth put the opera cape back in the box. And the next day she looked into the same closet, found that the same box had been torn open again and the opera cape removed. She went right up to Kenneth's room. He wasn't there, but sure enough the opera cape was hanging up in his closet. So Agnes took it down and put it back in the box. And the next day——"

"Don't say it," Mom said.

"You're right," I said. "The opera cape was gone. It was too much for Agnes. She didn't want to spend all her time running after that opera cape. So she told herself Kenneth probably wanted it for some innocent game of his, and she shrugged off the whole thing.

"But Kenneth's stealing didn't stop there. Only two days later—about three days ago—he was at it again. The housemaid came to Agnes in great alarm, along with the cook. The night before, they had both heard strange noises coming from the top floor of the house. They both thought it was mice or the wind or something, and went to sleep. But this morning, when the housemaid went upstairs to clean, she found a terrible disorder that neither mice nor wind could have caused. There's a small storeroom on the top floor, and in this storeroom, packed away in mothballs, Agnes keeps all of her late husband's uniforms, his caps, his insignia, the rest of his civilian clothes, overcoats, shoes, and so on. The housemaid found this room looking as if a cyclone had hit it. Clothes and mothballs were scattered all over the place. And all her husband's uniforms, down to the last little insignia, were missing. The cook immediately announced that she was quitting her job. She wasn't going to stay in the same house with a wild little thief like Kenneth, and all Agnes's pleading wouldn't change her mind.

71

MY MOTHER, THE DETECTIVE

"Well, Agnes just didn't know what to make out of all this. She was really worried about the boy by now, so worried that she thought of taking him to a doctor or a child psychologist to find out what was wrong. But she isn't a very decisive person. She put off calling the doctor, and then yesterday morning it was too late. Yesterday morning the murder happened."

I could see the gleam of interest in Mom's eye. A certain perverse something in my nature made me pause, sigh, chew my food, and generally encourage the atmosphere of suspense.

Finally, to my immense satisfaction, Mom spoke up. "All right, all right, not so much *geschrei* and get to the point!"

"Yesterday morning," I went on, "right from the start Kenneth acted funny. He had breakfast as usual with his mother and his Uncle Nelson. Only Kenneth, who was ordinarily a big eater at breakfast, wouldn't touch a bit of food—not even a glass of water.

"After breakfast he went off to play. He had a favorite spot for his games, a small canvas canopy set up on the roof of the house. This was Kenneth's 'clubhouse'—but until Nelson's arrival, he didn't have any other 'club member' to go with it. So now, after breakfast, he went up to the roof with his Uncle Nelson. Only Kenneth didn't go up with his usual energy and high spirits. He climbed the stairs to the roof in a slow trudging way, glancing back over his shoulder, and with a sort of determined look on his face. His mother saw him on the way and wondered about it, but she was busy on the phone at that moment, so she put it out of her mind.

"Two hours later she heard the yell. A long agonized yell. The whole household heard it, and even though it was hard to tell exactly where it came from, everybody instinctively made for the roof. When they got there they found Kenneth standing by the ledge—a narrow stone ledge as high as his chin—looking down at the backyard four stories below. He was looking at his Uncle Nelson. Apparently Nelson had fallen from the roof, and his body was lying on the concrete below. They all rushed downstairs to help him, of course, and they found that he was still alive. Only for a few more seconds, though. During those few seconds, in his last painful breath, he kept repeating the same words, 'Kenny, why? Kenny, why?' Then he died.

"Only one more thing to tell you, Mom. When the Homicide Squad arrived, we made a search of that roof. Underneath the canvas canopy, Kenneth's 'clubhouse,' we found—you guessed it, Mom —all those things Kenneth had stolen from the house. His father's uniforms, his father's opera cape, his father's insignia, even his father's Silver Star, which that kid had managed to sneak out of his mother's dresser for the second time!"

My voice came to a stop on a rising note. Frankly, I was pleased with myself. Very dramatically presented, I told myself. Now let Mom make sense out of this one!

"And the little boy?" Mom said, in a low voice.

"He went into a kind of shock," I said. "He grabbed hold of his mother and sobbed wildly for the rest of the day. But he won't say what happened up there on the roof. He just stares ahead when anybody asks him. The doctor says he'll get over the shock in a week or so. But after that his memory of the incident may be gone."

"And your opinion, Davie?" Mom said. "According to you and the police, what *did* happen on the roof?"

"It's not according to us, Mom. It's according to the facts. There are lots of different possibilities—we've considered them all—but only one of them seems to fit all the facts."

"So let's hear your possibilities."

"One possibility is that Nelson committed suicide. But this doesn't make sense. He was upset over being sick and leaving the Air Force, of course. But Agnes says he was just beginning to get *over* his illness, and to reconcile himself to civilian life. If he was going to kill himself because of his illness, why did he wait so long to do it? And what makes even less sense, why did he kill himself in the presence of his five-year-old nephew? People don't usually want witnesses to their suicides."

"Absolutely, I agree. Next possibility?"

"That Nelson's death was an accident. He was running, looking the wrong way, or something, and he tripped and fell over the ledge. But this is very unlikely. The ledge of the roof reached well above

73

Nelson's waist. It's hard to imagine any sort of purely accidental force that would tumble him over so high a ledge."

"A good point. I'm applauding."

"Well, there's the possibility—after all, we have to consider every-thing—that Nelson tried to push his little nephew Kenneth off the ledge, that Kenneth kicked and struggled and knocked Nelson over instead. But this doesn't fit the facts, either. When Agnes got to the roof, Kenneth was neat as a pin—no sign at all of a struggle, nor any sign of physical exertion. Which leaves us with only one other possibility."

"And this is?"

"I mentioned it already, Mom. We hate to believe it. We're fighting against believing it. But the facts leave us no alternative. That little five-year-old kid must be mentally unbalanced. It's hap-pened before, you know. Our official psychiatrist says he's come across dozens of cases of childhood psychosis, split personality, melan-cholia, and so on. So that's what it must be in this case. The death of his father, his lonely life, his dependence on his mother, the sudden arrival of his uncle to disrupt his routine—all this must have upset his feeling of security. It must have preyed on the kid's mind, and finally something snapped.

"The kid's crazy behavior before the murder tells us very clearly what was going on in his mind. By some peculiar twist—really not so peculiar—his uncle suddenly appeared to him as the rival of his dead father. His uncle was trying to take his father's place, and he, little Kenneth, had to prevent this for his father's sake. He had to get rid of this intruding uncle, remove the cause of his unhappiness, see to it that he and his father had his mother to themselves again.

"He didn't act the way an adult would, of course. It was just instinctive—the way a child steals or lies or kicks his nurse. But he did change his attitude toward his uncle. He pretended to feel affec-tion for him. He pretended to worship him like a hero. Then, when he had completely gained his uncle's trust, he got ready for the big moment. Which brings us to the most interesting psychological phe-nomenon. Little Kenneth was now going to do his father's work, and so, with typical childish logic, he proceeded to steal his father's things.

His father's uniforms, his father's opera cape, his father's medal—he took them all, slept on them or hid them away, in order to give himself his father's courage, his father's strength. By the time yesterday morning arrived, that poor kid had pushed himself into a real father fixation. In his own subconscious mind, he actually *was* his father.

"That's why he went up to the roof yesterday morning looking so determined. He had made up his mind what he was going to do. Once up there, he played with his uncle innocently for a while—the craftiness of little kids is really amazing, Mom! Finally, under some pretext, he persuaded his uncle to lean over the ledge. Remember that Nelson, even though he was a grown man, was weak and underweight and sick. Kenneth simply had to run up behind him, grab Nelson, lift, and then give him a push—the hardest push he could manage. Nelson toppled and screamed, and Kenneth went into shock.

"That's the story, Mom. And you can see another thing about it —it's the only theory that accounts for Nelson's last words. 'Why, Kenny, why?' Stunned, bewildered—even in his death throes, he just couldn't understand what had come over his little nephew."

"And this is your solution to the case?"

I nodded my head solemnly. "I'm afraid it is, Mom."

Mom was silent. She was looking thoughtful, abstracted, far away from our conversation and the dining room. This is peculiar behavior for Mom. On Friday nights, when I tell her about my latest case, she usually maintains a sharp, scornful attention. No sooner am I finished with my story than she pops out with cryptic questions, mysterious hints, sarcastic references to my thickheadedness. And finally, with great relish, she presents me with a complete, logical, inescapable solution based on her everyday experiences with scheming butchers, nosey neighbors, and selfish relatives. And so, this sudden frowning silence from Mom made me wonder.

A second later Mom's unusual mood vanished. Her head snapped up, a gleam of triumph was in her eye, and her voice sounded as vigorous as ever. "He's afraid it is. He *should* be afraid. He's got something to be afraid about. The whole police force of

New York City—a bunch of grown-up men with pensions coming to them any day now—and all they can think of when they got a body on their hands is to blame it on a little five-years-old boy!"

I felt a pang of hurt pride. "I've given you all the facts, Mom. Who do *you* want to blame it on?"

"I'll tell you," Mom said, "right after you answer me three simple questions."

I sighed. Mom's "simple questions" are well known to me. Generally they're so "simple" that they leave me ten times more confused than I was before. "Ask away, Mom," I said.

"Question One," she said, raising her forefinger. "This little boy, Kenny—did he go in much for games? Was he the athletical type?"

"Oh, I see why you're asking that," I said. "You want to know if he was really strong and agile enough to push his Uncle Nelson off the roof. Well, the answer doesn't prove much. The kid didn't go in much for athletics, because he didn't have many friends. In the neighborhood where he lives, it just happens that most of the kids are older. He was too small to play games with them—in fact, that may be one reason for his shyness and loneliness. On the other hand, he's a husky kid for his five years. Strong muscles, lots of stamina, excellent health. And his Uncle Nelson, as I pointed out, was sick and rundown—"

"Yes, yes, this I know." Mom interrupted impatiently. "Now, Question Two." She raised two fingers this time. "Little Kenny, what sort of books did he read?"

"Books, Mom?"

"Books, books. You remember, what you used to open up now and then when you was at college though God knows, with the crazy profession you decided to go into, you certainly didn't need them much. This little Kenny was shy and lonely, you said. He spent a lot of time by himself. So little boys like that, usually they do a lot of reading."

"I don't see the point of the question," I said, "but you're right. The kid is a big reader. His room was full of books. Comic books mostly. Superman, Batman, space travel, that sort of thing. He's a little too young yet for anything better."

MOM SHEDS A TEAR

"Good, good," Mom said, nodding her head. "Question Three. This is the most important question of all." She fixed her eyes on me hard for a moment, then brought it out: "Yesterday, when Uncle Nelson got killed, it was late in the morning. I was busy in the meat market all morning—a little misunderstanding over my lamb chops, which I had a discussion about with Perelman the butcher—so I didn't notice what the weather was like outside. Was it nice and sunny, or was it dark and cloudy?"

I just stared at her. "*That's* the most important question of all? Mom, what's the point of it?"

"Never mind the point. Only give me an answer."

"It was a bright sunny day yesterday. The hottest day so far this summer. But I don't see—"

"You don't," Mom said. "But I do." Then she nodded her head and went back to her food.

After a while I cleared my throat. "You do what, Mom?"

"I see. Exactly what I suspected. Exactly the solution that was in my head right at the beginning."

"You mean the little boy had nothing to do with it?"

"Who said so? The little boy had everything to do with it." Mom enjoyed my confusion for a few moments, then she gave a sigh and a shake of her head. "Davie, Davie, don't you see the mistake you was making all along, you and the Homicide Squad? All this talk about little boys that want their Mama's affection, and they're jealous of their uncles, and they get a Papa fixation and steal things and it's just like kicking the nurse—this is very clever, only it isn't what goes on inside the head of a little boy. It's only what you personally think *ought* to go on inside the head of a little boy."

"And you know what does go on inside a little boy's head, Mom?"

"Why shouldn't I? For a lot of years didn't I have a little boy's head right under my nose here in this apartment? A lot of *tsouris* it gave me, that head, but believe me I found out what went on inside of it. And you yourself, you and Shirley, you could find this out too. If you stopped reading psychology books for a minute and— All right, all right, no propaganda, back to the case. The main thing you should remember about a five-years-old boy is that he's only five

77

years old. Only five years he's been alive in this world, and half that time he was learning how to talk English.

"So how much can you expect such a little baby to find out about life in five years? What's true, what isn't true? If you put your finger into a candle flame, you get a burn. But you put your finger into a sunbeam, and it only feels nice and warm. So how can a little baby find out the difference till he tries it for himself? When Papa comes home, you can throw your arms around his neck and kiss him on the cheek. But what about the nice man on the television set—how come you can't throw your arms around him and kiss *his* cheek? Mama tells you a fairy story before you go to sleep—you hear Papa talking about a story from the newspapers about a little boy who got kidnaped. So which one of these stories is true? Which one is only for fun, and which one should you be frightened at? Which one of them really happened? Is there anything in this world that couldn't happen?

"It's like my baby brother Max, your Uncle Max, when he was seven years old and we came to America. Ever since he could remember, Max heard about the gangsters in America. Only what was a gangster? How old was a gangster? Did he look like other people? Anybody bigger than Max, who shouted at him and hit him, anybody like that, for Max at age seven could be a gangster. And wasn't it his bad luck, the first neighborhood we moved into, near Delancey Street, to meet a couple little boys ten years old that wasn't exactly the sweetest, kindest little boys in the world? So he asked them one day, 'What's a gangster, Sammy? Are you a gangster, Charlie?' So Sammy and Charlie winked at each other and said, 'Absolutely, we're a couple of gangsters, we're the worst gangsters in the whole city. We've got big guns in our pockets right now, and we're going to shoot you.'

"And didn't poor little Max believe them? Naturally he believed them. For weeks and weeks he was scared to death of them. He hid his face whenever a policeman passed by. He lost his appetite. He hated to step out of the house. And one time, when they told him they were going to come into his room in the middle of the night and kill him, he laid awake shivering in his bed, and when he heard the door squeak he jumped practically out of the window. Believe me, if the window had been opened a little farther, my brother Max wouldn't be your Uncle Max today."

"Mom, this is ridiculous," I broke in. "Are you saying that little Kenneth talked his Uncle Nelson into believing that he was a gangster, that a five-year-old kid scared a grown man into jumping off the roof?"

"Certainly I'm not saying this!" Mom drew herself up with dignity. "All I'm saying is—little children are so small and ignorant, they've got such a trust in people, such a willingness to believe anything you tell them, they're like little delicate china knickknacks that you keep on the hall table. They're so weak, and the rest of the world is so big and strong and clumsy, and cruel sometimes, that there's practically a million ways to break them into a million pieces."

"I still don't get it—"

"What I'm saying is this, Davie. If you wanted to get rid of a five-years-old boy, if he was in your way or you didn't like him, you wouldn't have to kill him and take the chance you'll get arrested for murder. You could be much smarter. You could work on him a little, tell him things, frighten him and confuse him, and eventually get him to do some crazy thing so he'd have an accident and get killed."

This statement stunned me. I didn't know how to take it. I felt there was a glimmer of meaning in Mom's words, but I couldn't quite see it.

"I'm talking, Davie," Mom said, "about all that stealing which little Kenny did. Nowadays there's so much talk from psychiatry, everybody you meet thinks he's another Dr. Sigmund Freed. Somebody does something we don't understand, so right away we say, 'Ha, Ha! It's psychiatrical! It's a Papa fixation! It's an infra-red complex!' But sometimes, Davie, things have got a simple, obvious explanation —if you only take a little trouble and look at them.

"This last week, before his Uncle Nelson gets killed, little Kenny spends all his time stealing his Papa's things. So naturally you come to the conclusion, he wants to take his Papa's place and get rid of his uncle. But one thing you're forgetting—little Kenny didn't just steal his Papa's things, he stole only certain *particular* things. When he tore open the box in the closet for his Papa's opera cape, he didn't touch his Papa's books or papers. When he went through the storeroom for his Papa's uniforms, he didn't bother about his Papa's civilian suits. When he opened up his Mama's case, he didn't take away his Papa's cufflinks, he only took his Papa's medal. So isn't this interesting that he only takes a certain type thing belonging to his Papa? His Papa's *uniform*, his Papa's *insignia*, his Papa's *medal*—he only takes things which are connected with his Papa's work as an Air Force pilot."

"Yes, that's true, Mom. But what does it prove? Besides," I added suddenly, "he took the opera cape! What does the opera cape have to do with the Air Force?"

"The opera cape is the whole answer, Davie. A little boy is interested in stealing everything that his Papa used in the Air Force—but he also steals his Papa's opera cape. He steals it once, twice, three times. Such anxiousness to get hold of this opera cape. What's it so important for? A little idea comes into my head, and I ask you the question: what books does he read? The answer is like I expected. Comic books—but which comic books? Cowboy books? Detective books? Pirate treasure books? No. This little Kenny, he's interested in other subjects. Space traveling, Superman, Batman. And Superman and Batman, when they go flying through the air, what is it that they're always wearing, streaming away behind them, sticking out from the wind?"

"A big long flowing cape!" I cried—and the light dawned.

"What else? So it isn't such a mixed-up *kasha* any more, is it? It's as clear as a consommé now. A common, normal, boyish thing was going on in little Kenny's head, a thing which lots of little boys go through, a thing which causes plenty little accidents and some big ones every year. Little Kenny got it into his head that he was going to fly!"

"Of course," I said, almost with a groan. "I should've seen it all along. I remember, one summer when I was six, three of us climbed a tree in Uncle Dan's backyard— But we lost our nerve at the last minute."

"This I never heard before," Mom said, giving me a sharp look. Then she shrugged. "And such a natural thing for little Kenny. His Papa used to be an Air Force pilot. Flying was a regular topic of conversation in his house. And his Papa was a hero to him. And he's a boy who don't have many friends. A strong active boy, but too small to play with the other boys in the neighborhood. They laugh at him maybe. They tell him to go away, he's a midget, what good could *he* be on the team? It's a terrible torture to him. What else does he want in this world except a chance to show them how wrong they are, to do something absolutely wonderful even though he *is* small, so that from then on they'll be happy to have him on the team?

"Yesterday morning was the big moment, like you say. He was looking determined when he went up to the roof—not because he was going to kill somebody, but because he was finally going to put on his long cape, and maybe also part of his Papa's uniform and his Papa's insignia, and fly off from the roof. This was why he wouldn't eat breakfast or drink any water. Because he wanted to be as light as he could—"

"I get it, Mom. And then, just as he was about to climb up on the ledge, his Uncle Nelson realized what was happening. He tried to stop the kid. He rushed at him. Kenneth sidestepped. Nelson lost his balance and fell off the roof instead."

"Almost," Mom said. "Not exactly. You forgot the most important detail. A little boy gets a crazy idea in his head. 'I can fly,' he says. 'I'll go up to the roof and try it.' But little Kenny didn't get this idea all of a sudden. He got it over a week ago. He stole his Papa's uniform because he knew his Papa could never fly without it, and he wanted its mysterious power to come to him. He stole Papa's medal and slept with it under his pillow, the way little children sleep on a tooth—so he could have his wish to fly in the air like Papa. He stole Papa's long opera cape for his wings. So clever, so psychiatrical—to me this means only one thing. Little Kenny didn't get the idea all by himself.

"Oh, yes, he was *ready* for the idea. This I admit. He was lonely, he was full of imagination, his big hero was his Papa the Air Force pilot. You and the Homicide Squad was closer than you thought,

MY MOTHER, THE DETECTIVE

Davie, when you said that the whole case depended on the little boy's feelings for his Papa. What you didn't see was that somebody had to work on these feelings. Stealing the uniforms, using the opera cape, sleeping on the medal—these are schemes which would appeal to a little boy, but which a five-years-old boy wouldn't be able to think up himself. Somebody else—"

"But who is this somebody, Mom? Agnes Fisher herself? I can't believe it. Such a pretty scatterbrained woman—and she really loves her son. One of the servants maybe? How about the cook, the one who suddenly quit a few days before the accident?"

Mom gave a snort. "Foolishness. A cook who ups and leaves, nowadays it's a common occurrence. It would be a miracle if the cook *didn't* up and leave. The answer isn't so complicated, Davie. Look at it this way. The big day is here. Little Kenny is going to fly. He's nervous. He eats no breakfast. He goes up to the roof like a criminal going to the electrical chair. Two hours he's up there, but he can't bring himself to get started. The person who's put this idea in his head, he don't dare go away until he's sure little Kenny is really going to jump. So finally he says to the boy, 'It's very simple. Here, I'll show you exactly how you begin. I'll climb up on the ledge. I'll flap my arms like a bird. I'll do everything except fly—which I couldn't do, because I'm too big and heavy—' "

"Wait a second, Mom! Are you saying that Nelson Fisher was behind his nephew's crazy behavior?"

"Who else? Who acted very peculiar for a grown man, ignoring the company of people his own age and spending his time with a little five-years-old? Who was lonely and sick and in a terrible state because his life as a plane pilot was over? Who could think to himself, 'This sister-in-law of mine likes me already. She could be mine along with her house and her money—if only this little brat was out of the way'? And who was it, after the first jealousy wore off, that had the most influence over little Kenny? Who did little Kenny hero-worship and believe everything he said—especially on the subject of flying, because wasn't his Uncle Nelson an Air Force pilot like his Papa used to be? And last but not littlest, who was up on the roof with little Kenny all morning? Nelson, exclusively Nelson, he climbed on the ledge, he flapped his arms, he shouted, 'Look, Kenny, see how easy it is? Why are you hesitating, Kenny? Why are you acting scared? *Why, Kenny, why?*'— and then he fell over himself."

The picture before my eyes fascinated me, kept me silent for a moment. Then I said, "But how did it happen, Mom? What made him lose his balance and fall from the ledge?"

Mom frowned. "This was a problem. For a while it bothered me. And then it came to me, and I asked you about the weather. It was a bright, hot, sunny morning, you said. So I put myself in this no-good Nelson's place. I'm excited. I'm so close to what I've been waiting and working for. And I'm a man who had malaria, a man who still gets dizzy spells. I climb up on a ledge—a narrow ledge, four stories up, and when I look down I see how far it is to the ground. And the sun is so hot, and it's beating down on me, I flap my arms, I yell at the little boy, then everything begins to dance in front of me. It's one of my dizzy spells. My God, I'm falling—I'm flying—" And Mom let her voice trail off solemnly.

After a pause, I laughed out loud, I couldn't help myself. "Mom, you don't know how grateful I am. A five-year-old murderer—we've been hating the idea all day. What a relief for the boys down at Homicide!"

"What a relief for the Mama," said Mom, in a low voice.

I looked at her a moment. And then I thought I'd have a little fun with her. "But you haven't proved your main point, Mom," I said, pretending to be very serious. "You still haven't proved that it's a good thing to have kids, that they aren't all little monsters."

Mom's head snapped up. "I haven't proved it? Who said so? Didn't I show you that this Kenny is a sweet, innocent, intelligent little child?"

"Yes, Mom. But what about Nelson? Nelson was somebody's child once."

"Nelson?" Mom gaped at me, almost at a loss for words. Then her voice grew very fierce. "Nelson don't mean nothing! What kind of talk is this, bringing up Nelson as an argument?"

"I don't know, Mom." I shrugged my shoulders elaborately. "Shirley and I will have to do a lot of thinking about this. We'd love to have a kid like Kenneth. But suppose that kid grew up to be like Nelson. It's quite a problem."

"It's no problem!" Mom shook her head back and forth energetically. "Don't talk like that—a son of mine! Don't get a prejudice against children, I beg you, Davie. Little children—little grandchildren they're the most beautiful thing in the world. Sometimes I think they're the *only* beautiful thing the world."

Then it happened—something I never thought I'd see. A mist came into Mom's eyes, a trembling over her lips, and while I stared in amazement, Mom shed a tear.

I was terribly ashamed of myself. "Please, Mom," I said, "I was only fooling."

She recovered herself instantly. She got to her feet, her eyes dry again. "So was I!" she snorted. Then she stamped out indignantly to fetch the nesselrode pie.

MOM MAKES A WISH

ORDINARILY MY WIFE SHIRLEY AND I HAVE DINner in the Bronx with my mother on Friday nights. This is the most convenient time for me, because Saturday is my day off from the Homicide Squad. Once a year, though, we show up even if it isn't Friday—since the night of December eighteenth is Mom's birthday.

Another hard-and-fast custom gets upset on this night. Mom doesn't do any of the work on the dinner. Shirley cooks it, and I wash the dishes, so that Mom can sit back in her easy chair and relax and enjoy the television or gossip with her friends over the telephone. She does this relaxing, of course, under protest. Her suspicion of Shirley's abilities as a cook is deep-rooted. "So where did you learn how to cook? Nowadays, the way they bring up the young girls, if she knows how to boil an egg she considers herself a regular Oscar of the Walgreen." And when Shirley explains about the Home Economics course she took at Wellesley, Mom simply gives one of her magnificent snorts.

"Wellesley yet! So answer me please, how good was the *gefuelte* fish at Wellesley?"

As for my dish-washing, Mom's opinion of it couldn't be lower. All she can do is throw up her hands and bemoan, "Once a *schlimazl* always a *schlimazl!*"

But Shirley and I have a stubborn streak of our own, so inevitably we win out over Mom's protests. And she usually has a pleasant birthday party in the end.

At last year's celebration there was a special treat. I brought along Inspector Millner. Inspector Millner is my superior, and also the most eligible bachelor on the Homicide Squad. He's a tall, thin man in his fifties, with grayish hair, a square tough jaw, and a curiously delicate melancholy look in his eyes which makes him very

85

attractive to motherly ladies of his own age. For a while now, Shirley and I have been trying a little mild matchmaking between Inspector Millner and Mom.

She was delighted to see him. She clapped him on the back and brought out all her heartiest jokes about policemen. He smiled sheepishly, enjoying his own embarrassment. And then, towards the middle of the meal, Mom suddenly gave him a shrewd sharp look.

"So why don't you finish your chicken leg?" she said. "It's a nice chicken—considering it wasn't cooked, it was home-economized. You got some worry on your mind, don't you?"

Inspector Millner attempted a smile. "You see right inside of a man, as usual," he said. "Okay, I admit it. David can tell you what it is."

"It's this new case we're on, Mom," I said. "A pretty depressing business."

"A mystery?" Mom said, cocking her head forward. The keen interest that Mom takes in my cases is surpassed only by her uncanny talent for solving them long before I can.

"No mystery," I said. "It's a murder, and we know who did it, and we'll probably make the arrest before the end of the week."

Inspector Millner heaved a long sad sigh.

"So come on, come on," Mom said, with extra cheerfulness. "Tell me all about this, spit it out of your chest."

I took a breath, and started in:

"First of all, you have to know about this college professor. This *ex*-professor, that is. Professor Putnam. He's a man over fifty now, and he lives in a small three-room walk-up apartment near Washington Square with his daughter Joan. Ten years ago Putnam used to teach English Literature at the college downtown. He was considered quite a brilliant man. Then his wife died, and he seems to have gone almost completely to seed. He would sit in his room for long periods of time, just staring at the ceiling. He showed up late for his classes—and after a while he stopped showing up at all. He wouldn't read his students' essays, and he began to skip his conferences with graduate students. He was warned several times by the Dean about his conduct, and because of his fine record and the tragedy in his life

86

great allowances were made for him. But finally, after two years of this, the college decided that they couldn't keep him on. So the Dean told him he was dismissed."

"And this daughter that you mentioned?" Mom said. "She was what age at this time?"

"She was seventeen," I said, "just starting at college herself. But when her father lost his job, she had to quit school. And since he wasn't doing anything to help himself, she found that she had the responsibility of supporting both of them. She learned typing and shorthand, and got a job as secretary in a law office, and she's been doing nicely ever since. They don't live in luxury, you understand."

"And the old man," Mom said, "he never snapped himself up again?"

With another long sigh, Inspector Millner took the story over from me. "He went from bad to worse, I'm afraid. Shortly after he lost his job, he took to drinking. Twice a week—every Thursday and Monday—he left the apartment after dinner and didn't come home till after midnight, reeking of whiskey, so drunk that he could hardly walk. Joan Putnam was always waiting up to put him to bed. Several times in the last ten years she's tried to break him of the habit, but with no success. Because in addition to his twice-a-week binges, he keeps bottles of whiskey hidden around the house. Every so often she finds one, a big full bottle of the cheapest stuff, and she throws it away. But he always manages to think of a new hiding place."

"And that's not the worst of it," I broke in. "When Professor Putnam lost his job, he blamed the Dean for it. Dean Duckworth was about his own age—the two men had started at the college together as young instructors and had been friends for many years. When Dean Duckworth told him he was dismissed, Professor Putnam made a terrific scene—it's still remembered by other people on the faculty. He accused the Dean of forcing him out of his job because of jealousy, of ruining his career, of bringing about his wife's death—of all sorts of things. He threatened to get even with him some day. And ever since, old Professor Putnam has gone on hating Dean Duckworth just as loudly and publicly as he did ten years ago. Recently, though, the whole business came to a head—"

"I think I can guess this head," Mom said. "Dean Ducksoup has got a young bachelor son, am I wrong?"

"Amazing," Inspector Millner murmured, under his breath. "We could use a brain like that on the Homicide Squad."

"For all practical purposes," Mom said, "you're already using it."

"Well, to get on with the story," I said quickly because even Inspector Millner doesn't know exactly to what extent Mom helps me out with my knottier cases. "You're absolutely right, Mom. Dean Duckworth's son Ted is an instructor at the college. He's in his early thirties and still unmarried. And a few months ago he became engaged to Joan Putnam. The engagement was perfectly satisfactory to Dean Duckworth. But Putnam raised a terrific row. He told his daughter that he refused to let her marry the son of the man who had ruined his life. He wouldn't let the boy set foot in his apartment when he came to make friends. And one night, a week ago, he stormed right into Dean Duckworth's home—the Dean has a two-story house off Washington Square—and made a scene in front of a room full of guests. He yelled out that Dean Duckworth had taken his job away from him, his wife away from him, his self-respect away from him, and now he was trying to rob him of the only thing he had left in the world, his daughter. He told the Dean that he was going to kill him for that. 'And it won't be murder,' he said, 'it'll be an execution.' The upshot of it all was that his daughter Joan told young Ted Duckworth that she couldn't go through with the marriage right now—she insisted on postponing it until her father sees reason."

"Which will be never," Shirley put in. "The case is really quite a common one. He justifies his neurotic dependence upon his daughter by transferring his feelings of guilt to a third party—"

"Very common," Mom put in, with that edge that always comes into her voice when Shirley pops out with her Wellesley psychology course. "What a big help to the people that's involved, to tell them that they're really quite a common case."

"Anyway, you can guess what happened, Mom," I went on. "Last Monday night after dinner, Professor Putnam left his apartment for his regular drunken binge. Joan waited up for him as usual. Only he wasn't in by midnight. He didn't get in till 1:30. He was staggering and reeking with whiskey, of course. And around the same time a policeman in the Washington Square area found Dean Duckworth's body. He was lying on the sidewalk about a block from his own house. He had been brutally beaten to death, and the weapon was right by the body—a broken whiskey bottle.

"Well, we were on the job all morning. We found out from his son and his wife that he had left his house around 12:30 to buy a late newspaper at the subway station. But he had no paper on him, and the news vendor didn't remember seeing him, so he must have met his murderer on the way. Mrs. Duckworth and Ted were together all night, incidentally, waiting for him to come home, so they alibi each other. We also found out, in no time at all, the whole background of his feud with Professor Putnam. By 6 o'clock in the morning we were at Professor Putnam's door, to question him about his whereabouts all night."

"The poor fellow," Inspector Millner said, shaking his head. "He was completely muddled and bleary-eyed. His daughter had a lot of trouble waking him up. When we told him what had happened to Dean Duckworth, he blinked at us for a while as if he couldn't understand what we were saying. Then he started crying. And then he started talking about the old days, the days when Duckworth and he were idealistic young men, starting off in the teaching profession together. And all the time his daughter, that poor kid, was staring back and forth from us to her father, with a kind of horror in her eyes because she knew what was coming."

"It was terrible, Mom," I said, shuddering a little at the memory. "Finally we had to interrupt him and ask him pointblank to account for his actions that night. Well, he refused to do it."

Mom narrowed her eyes at this. "He refused? Or he couldn't remember because he'd been drinking so much?"

"He refused. He didn't even claim he couldn't remember. He just said that he wouldn't tell us. We warned him how incriminating it looked, and his daughter pleaded with him. She said that he didn't have to be ashamed if he was in a bar drinking somewhere because everybody knew about his habit anyway. But he still refused. Well, what could we do, Mom? We didn't exactly charge him with murder yet, but we took him down to headquarters for questioning."

Mom nodded wisely. "Third degree."

"No, not third degree," I answered, a little annoyed. Even though she knows better, Mom likes to pretend that the police department is still using the methods they used a hundred years ago. This is Mom's idea of making fun of me. "Nobody laid a finger on him. But we did question him pretty thoroughly, on and off, for over twelve hours."

"We have to do it that way," Inspector Millner put in apologetically. "Murderers are pretty jumpy usually, right after their crime. The sooner we get to them and work at them, the better chance there is of getting a confession. Don't think I enjoyed it," he added hastily. "That poor old man—really old, though he's actually the same age as I am—God knows I didn't enjoy it."

Mom's voice and face softened immediately. "Of course you didn't enjoy it," she said to Inspector Millner. "I'm a dope if I even hinted that you did."

"And the point is," I said, "Professor Putnam *didn't* confess. He insisted he hadn't committed the murder, but he refused to tell us where he was at the time. Well, we didn't really have enough evidence yet to hold him, so we took him back to his home and his daughter."

Inspector Millner reddened slightly. "She had some pretty strong things to say to us, I'm afraid." He sighed. "Well, a policeman gets used to it—"

"We were pretty sure Putnam was guilty," I said, "so our next step was to find witnesses who could place him in the neighborhood that night. Naturally it wasn't hard. When a man goes out on a drunk—even if he's like Putnam, and prefers to do it alone, without drinking companions—sure enough somebody is bound to notice him. We went to all the bars in the vicinity of the house and showed Putnam's photograph around. Finally we got results at a bar only three blocks from the Duckworth house. Harry Sloan, the bartender and also the owner of the place, remembered Putnam. He'd seen Putnam in his place off and on during the last few years. And the night of the murder, he saw Putnam again. It was around a quarter of one in the morning. Harry and his wife were closing the place up—they do their business mostly with the college kids, and since this is vacation time they take the opportunity to close up shortly after midnight and get some sleep. Well, Putnam came knocking on the door, making a terrible ruckus. They opened the door and told him they were closed, but he insisted he had to have a drink, and he showed them the money to pay for it. Harry figured it would be easier to give him what he wanted and then send him away. So he let Putnam in, and Harry and his wife say that the old man killed nearly half a bottle of bourbon before they could get rid of him at a quarter past one. He wasn't just drinking for the pleasure of it, they say. He really seemed to have something on his mind. Mrs. Sloan says he looked scared of something to her."

"So this don't prove he committed a murder."

"No. But along with everything else it's pretty strong evidence. First of all, he had the motive. Second of all, he had the opportunity. The time schedule is just right. Duckworth leaves his house at 12:30 to get a paper. On the way—by accident or on purpose—he's met by Putnam. Putnam is carrying a bottle, which he uses to hit Duckworth. That's around a quarter of one. Putnam is then so upset and scared at what he's done that he makes for the nearest bar, desperate for a drink. He leaves the bar at a quarter past one, and gets home, by his daughter's own testimony, at 1:30. Third of all, his behavior fits in perfectly with this theory—his urgent need for a drink in Sloan's bar, his refusal to tell us what he was doing all night. It's an open-and-shut case, Mom."

And Inspector Millner joined in mournfully. "Open-and-shut. There's no other way to look at the evidence."

There was a long silence, and then Mom produced a snort. "There's *one* other way," she said. "The *right* way!"

We all lifted our heads and stared at her. How many times has Mom done this to me—but every time she takes me by surprise!

"Really, Mother," Shirley was the first one to react, "you *can't* mean that you've got some *other* solution—"

"Now you're kidding, Mom," I said.

91

"Impossible, impossible," said Inspector Millner, shaking his head.. "I wish it could be—that poor old man, but it's impossible."

"We'll see how impossible," Mom said. "Only first I'd like to ask three simple questions."

I tightened up a little. Mom's "simple questions" have a way of confusing things beyond all understanding—until Mom herself shows how simple and relevant those questions really are. "Go ahead and ask them," I said, in a wary voice.

"Question One: A little bit of information please about this Dean Duckpond. What was his opinion of Professor Putnam being such a big drunk? Of drunkenness did he approve or disapprove?"

I had been afraid the question wouldn't make any sense, but I answered patiently all the same. "He didn't approve at all," I said. "Dean Duckworth was a big teetotaler—he was running a crusade against college students drinking, and trying to pass rules, and so forth. He used to tell his wife and his son that Putnam's taking to drink was proof of his weak moral character. It showed how right Duckworth had been to fire him from his job ten years ago."

Mom beamed with satisfaction. "That's a good answer," she said. "Question Two: When you got through giving Professor Putnam his third degree down at police headquarters and you then took him home to his daughter, what did he do?"

"What did he do, Mom?"

"I'm the one that's asking."

Again it didn't seem to make any sense, but again I was patient. "As a matter of fact, we know what he did, Mom, because we kept a man in the apartment to make sure Putnam didn't try to skip out. He went to sleep on the couch, right in front of his daughter and our man. The next morning he woke up and had breakfast. Orange juice, toast, and coffee. Two lumps of sugar. Is that an important clue?"

Mom ignored my sarcasm and went on beaming. "It's a clue if you got the brains to see it. Final Question: Is it possible that one of the movie houses in the neighborhood was playing *Gone With the Wind* on the night of the murder?"

This was too much for me. "Honestly, Mom. This is a murder investigation, not a joke!" And Shirley and Inspector Millner also made sounds of bewilderment.

"So who's joking?" Mom answered serenely. "Do I get my answer?"

It was Inspector Millner who answered, in a voice of respect. "I don't see how it fits in," he said, "but as a matter of fact, the neighboring Loew's *was* playing *Gone With the Wind*. I remember passing it on my way to question Professor Putnam for the first time."

"Exactly like I thought," Mom said, with her nod of triumph. "The case is now sewed in the bag."

"That's very interesting, Mother," Shirley said, as sweet as she could. "'But of course, David and Inspector Millner *already* have the case sewed in the—sewed up, that is. They know who the murderer is, and they're ready to arrest him."

"Whether we like it or not," Inspector Millner muttered.

But Mom's look of triumph wasn't disturbed a bit. She simply turned it on Inspector Millner, and a touch of tenderness mingled in it. "Maybe you'll end up liking it," she said. "Professor Putnam didn't do the murder."

Again we all stared at her.

Inspector Millner blinked uncertainly—half relieved, and half unwilling to believe in his relief. "Do you—you honestly have some proof of that?"

"It's such a simple thing," Mom said, spreading her hands. "It's my cousin Millie the Complainer all over again."

"Your cousin Millie—?" Inspector Millner's relief began to waver.

"The Complainer," Mom said, with a nod. "Never did she stop complaining, that woman. Always about her health. Her heart was weak. Her legs hurt. She had a pain in her back. Her stomach wasn't digesting. Her head was giving a headache. A physical wreck she was—every year a *different* kind of a physical wreck. She wasn't married either, and her poor brother Morris, her younger brother, he lived with her and supported her. He never got married either. If he so much as looked once at a girl, cousin Millie's aches would start aching separate and all together, harder than ever. One day she died. She was climbing on a chair up to the kitchen cupboard to get for herself a piece of cheesecake, and she lost her step, and hit her head on the floor, and the concussion killed her. When the doctor examined her, he told her brother Morris that, except for the bump on her head, she was absolutely the healthiest corpse he ever saw. Only by that time poor Morris was already fifty-seven years old, with a bald head and a pot belly that no woman would look at."

Mom stopped talking, and we all thought hard.

Finally Shirley said, "Mother, I just don't see the connection."

"The connection," Mom said, "it's right in front of your nose. It was the timing that gave me first an inkling of it."

"The timing, Mom?"

"The timing of this Professor Putnam. He's a drunk, you told me, who goes out every Thursday night and every Monday, always at the same time, always after dinner, and always he comes in at the same time, around midnight, staggering a little and smelling from whiskey. Right away this to me is peculiar. A drunk who keeps such regular hours, on a schedule almost, like a businessman. When a man gets drunk—extra special drunk like this Professor—he don't look at his watch so careful. Chances are he couldn't see his watch even if he looked at it. Besides which, this timing of his—Thursdays and Mondays from after dinner to midnight—this reminds me of something else. This reminds me of the schedule at a movie house. On Thursday and Monday the picture changes, and the complete double bill runs from after dinner till before midnight."

"Mom," I broke in, "do you mean—?"

"Quiet," Mom said. "You didn't see it from the beginning, so you got to give me the pleasure of telling it at the end. The timing makes me suspicious so I ask you a question: After he left the police head-quarters, where he was questioned for twelve hours, what did this Professor Putnam do? He went home, he went to bed and slept, he woke up and had breakfast. He didn't have a single drink! Not once even did he ask for a drink! A man who's supposed to be a regular drunk, and who's just been twelve hours with the third degree—he isn't even interested in taking a drink afterwards? Excuse me, this isn't sensible. So my original suspicion is positively proved—"

"He wasn't a drunkard at all," said Inspector Millner in a voice of wonder.

"Absolutely," Mom said. "Chances are he didn't even like the stuff. He was only *pretending* at being a drunk. Every Thursday night and Monday night for ten years, out he goes to the new show at the neighborhood movie house. He stays there till the show is over. Then he buys himself a bottle of whiskey maybe, he soaks his collar and his hands with it, he comes home and staggers for his daughter's benefit. Add on to this—he hides whiskey bottles around the house— always full whiskey bottles; his daughter, you notice, don't ever find any half-empty whiskey bottles. Also add on to this that he's very careful to explain that he's a lonely drunk, he don't ever have any companions to drink with."

"But why?" I said. "Why did, he fool his daughter that way all these years?"

"My cousin Millie the Complainer." Mom said, with a smile. "This Professor loses his job, also he loses his manliness, he loses his grip on life. His daughter comes to take care of him, and he's happy to let her. But always he's afraid some day she'll get married and leave him. He needs something besides his own weakness to keep her with him. So he turns himself into a drunk. How can a nice kind-hearted affectionate daughter go away and leave a poor drunk father all by himself? And it works. It works with poor Joan just like it worked with my poor cousin Morris. Only this time maybe it's not too late."

We were all silent for a while. In our minds we saw the picture of that broken old man, with still enough craftiness in him to plot holding on to his daughter. "And he was so ashamed of himself," Inspector Millner said, "that he preferred to face a murder charge than to admit that he *hadn't* been out drinking on Monday night."

"Just a minute," Shirley spoke up sharply. "You said he always went to the movies on Monday night, Mother, and that's why he always got home around midnight—the length of a double feature, you said. But on the night of the murder he didn't get home till 1:30. Now doesn't that prove that he committed the murder after all?"

Mom laughed. "You don't remember my final question. It proves only what I thought—that *Gone With the Wind* was playing at the neighborhood movie houses. And *Gone With the Wind* takes a good hour longer than the average double feature."

Shirley subsided, looking rather squelched.

"And now," Mom said, "we're all finished with the main course. So isn't somebody going to bring in the dessert? If I'm not running things myself—"

"I'll get it, Mom," I said. I rose to my feet and started to the kitchen door. But I was stopped by Shirley's voice.

"Wait!" Shirley turned to Mother with satisfaction. "You haven't really given us a solution to the crime at all. So Professor Putnam wasn't really a drunk. That doesn't tell us who *did* commit the murder."

"Don't it?" Mom smiled slyly. "It tells us absolutely and positively. Professor Putnam wasn't a drunk. We know this for a fact. So how, please, could he go into Harry Sloan's bar after closing time and drink up half a bottle of bourbon? And how, please, could Harry Sloan and his wife have seen him in that bar off and on for the last few years?"

Inspector Millner and I looked up sharply at this. And a determined, grim look came over the Inspector's face. "Sloan and his wife were lying?" he said.

"What else? This Sloan, he killed Dean Duckling himself. You told me his motive yourself. The Dean was a big crusader against drinking. He was trying to pass rules that the college students couldn't drink. This meant that the college students would go to bars that were far away from the college, so the Dean wouldn't catch them. And like you told me, this Sloan did most of his business with college students. The Dean was going to ruin his business—a pretty good motive to kill somebody in this day and age. Even so, in my opinion he didn't plan it out. He was on the street Monday night, and the Dean came by, going for his newspaper. And Sloan was maybe a little drunk himself and had a bottle with him. So he

96

stopped the Dean and he tried to argue him out of his crusade maybe, and one word led to another, and all of a sudden he's killed him. So back he goes and tells his wife—"

"And the next night," I said, with a groan, *"we* came along and gave him his big opportunity. We showed him Putnam's picture, and told him that Putnam had no alibi for the time of the murder—so Sloan and his wife thought it was safe to be the witnesses against him."

"And they would've got away with it," Inspector Millner said solemnly, "if it hadn't been for—" He broke off in a small flurry of embarrassment and admiration. Shirley and I exchanged our usual significant glance.

Shortly after, Inspector Millner got up and phoned headquarters to pick up Sloan and his wife. And I went out to the kitchen and lit the candles on Shirley's cake. Three candles—one for Mom's real age, one for the age she admitted to, and one for good luck. Then I marched the cake in, and we all sang "Happy Birthday To You," and Mom blushed prettily.

Then the cake was put in front of her, and Shirley and I shouted for her to make a wish and blow out the candles.

But she hesitated, with a look at Inspector Millner. "You're still feeling bad about something," she said.

"I'm sorry," he said, looking up and grinning, "I just can't seem to stop thinking about that poor old man. His daughter will find out the truth now, and then she'll be leaving to get married. What will happen to him when he's all alone?"

There was a touch of urgency in Inspector Millner's voice. And Mom's reply was curious. She ignored the question completely, and said in her positive voice, "Old! Who's old?"

Then, as if she had said something a little too revealing, she turned quickly to the cake. "First a wish and then a blow," she said shut her eyes tightly, and her lips moved soundlessly for a moment. Then she opened her eyes, leaned over the cake, and gave a blow.

Whatever it was that Mom wished she wasn't talking about it—not that night, anyway.

97

MOM SINGS AN ARIA

IT WAS ONE OF THE GREATEST DISAPPOINTMENTS of my mother's life that I never turned out to be a musical genius. For a couple of years, when I was a kid, Mom made me take violin lessons. At the end of the first year I played a piece called *Rustling Leaves*. At the end of the second year I was still playing *Rustling Leaves*. Poor Mom had to admit I wasn't another Jascha Heifitz, and that was the end of my musical career.

Mom has always been crazy about music herself. She did a little singing when she was a girl, and might have done something with her voice—instead she got married, moved up to the Bronx, and devoted herself to raising a future lieutenant in the New York City Homicide Squad. But she still listens regularly to the Saturday afternoon broadcasts of the Metropolitan Opera, and she can still hum along with all the familiar arias. That was why—when my wife Shirley and I went up to the Bronx the other night for our regular Friday dinner—I knew Mom would be interested in my latest case.

"You're a music lover, Mom," I said. "Maybe you can understand how a man could love music so much that he'd commit murder for it!"

"This is hard to understand?" Mom said, looking up from her roast chicken. "Why else did I stop your violin lessons? Once, while you were playing one of your pieces, I happened to take a look at your teacher, Mrs. Steinberg—and on her face was murder, if I ever saw it!"

"You don't mean that literally, do you, Mother?" Shirley said. "A woman wouldn't *really* feel like murdering a little boy because he played the violin badly."

"People can have plenty feelings that were never in your psychology books at college," Mom said. "Believe me, in my own family

—my Aunt Goldie who thought the pigeon outside her window was actually her late husband Jake—"

Mom went into detail, and her story was fascinating. Then she passed the chicken a second time, and I was able to get back to my murder.

"Have you ever seen the standing-room line at the Metropolitan Opera House?" I said. "Half an hour before every performance the box office sells standing-room tickets at two-fifty each, on a first-come first-served basis. The opera lovers start lining up outside the house hours ahead of time. They stand on their feet for three hours *before* the opera just so they can stand on their feet for three hours *during* the opera! Talk about crazy human motives!"

"People with no ears in their heads," Mom said, "shouldn't be so quick to call other people crazy." And she gave me one of those glares which has been making me feel like a naughty little five-year-old ever since I *was* a naughty little five-year-old.

I turned my eyes away and pushed on. "Well, there are certain people who show up on the opera standing-room line night after night, for practically every performance throughout the season. These 'regulars' are almost always at the head of the line—they come earlier than anyone else, wait longer, and take the best center places once they get inside the house. And since most of them have been doing this for years, they know each other by name, and they pass the time gossiping about the opera singers and discussing the performances. You could almost say they've got an exclusive little social club all their own—only their meeting place isn't a clubhouse, it's the sidewalk in front of the Met. Anyway, you couldn't imagine a more harmless collection of old fogeys—the last group on earth where you'd expect to find a murderer!"

"Even an opera lover has to have a private life," Mom said. "He enjoys himself with the beautiful music—but he's still got business troubles or love troubles or family troubles waiting for him at home."

"That's just it, Mom. If one of these standing-room regulars had gone home and killed his wife or his mother-in-law or his business partner, this would just be a routine case. But what happened was, he killed one of the other people in the standing-room line."

MY MOTHER, THE DETECTIVE

Mom was looking at me with her eyes narrowed—a sure sign that I had her interested. "The two oldest regulars in the standing-room line," I said, "the charter members of the club, are Sam Cohen and Giuseppe D'Angelo. Cohen used to be a pharmacist, with his own drug store on West Eighty-third Street. He retired fifteen years ago, after his wife died, and turned the management of the store over to his nephew, though he went on living in the apartment above it. As soon as he retired, he started going to the opera almost every night of the season.

"D'Angelo was in the exterminating business out in Queens—insects, rodents, and so on—but *he* retired fifteen years ago too. His wife is alive, but she doesn't care for music, so he's been in the habit of going to the Opera by himself—almost every night of the season, like Cohen.

"The two old men met on the standing-room line fifteen years ago and have seen each other three or four nights a week ever since—but only at the opera, never anywhere else. As far as we know, they've never met for a drink or a lunch, they've never been to each other's homes, and they've never seen each other at all in the summer, when the opera is closed.

"Opera is the biggest thing in both their lives. Cohen's mother was a vocal coach back in Germany, and he cut his teeth on operatic arias—D'Angelo was born and brought up in the city of Parma, which is the most operatic city in Italy—"

"I've read about Parma," Mom said. "If a tenor hits a bad note there, they run him out of town."

"How horrible!" Shirley said. "It's positively uncivilized!"

Mom shrugged. "A little less civilization here in New York, and maybe we wouldn't hear so many bad notes."

I could see the cloud of indignation forming on Shirley's face—she never *has* caught on to Mom's peculiar sense of humor. I hurried on, "Well, the two old men both loved opera, but their opinions about it have always been diametrically opposed. So for fifteen years they've been carrying on a running argument. If Cohen likes a certain soprano, D'Angelo can't stand her. If D'Angelo mentions having heard Caruso sing *Aida* in 1920, Cohen says that Caruso never sang *Aida* till 1923.

"And the old men haven't conducted these arguments in nice soft gentlemanly voices either. They yell at each other, wave their arms, call each other all sorts of names. 'Liar' and 'moron' are about the tamest I can think of. In spite of their bitterness, of course, these fights have never lasted long—before the fight is over, or at least by the time of the next performance, the old men always make it up between them—"

"Until now?" Mom said.

"I'll get to that in a minute, Mom. Just a little more background first. According to the other regulars on the standing-room line, the fights between Cohen and D'Angelo have become even more bitter than usual in recent years. They've been aggravated by a controversy which has been raging among opera lovers all over the world. Who's the greatest soprano alive today—Maria Callas or Renata Tebaldi?"

Mom dropped her fork and clasped her hands to her chest, and on her face came that ecstatic, almost girlish look which she reserves exclusively for musical matters. "Callas! Tebaldi! Voices like angels, both of them! That Callas—such fire, such passion! That Tebaldi —such beauty, such sadness! To choose which one is the greatest —it's as foolish as trying to choose between noodle soup and borscht!"

"Cohen and D'Angelo made their choices, though," I said. "D'Angelo announced one day that Tebaldi was glorious and Callas had a voice like a rooster—so right away Cohen told him that Callas was divine and Tebaldi sang like a cracked phonograph record. And the argument has been getting more and more furious through the years.

"A week ago a climax was reached. Callas was singing *Traviata*, and the standing-room line started to form even earlier than usual. Cohen and D'Angelo, of course, were right there among the first. Cohen had a bad cold—he was sneezing all the time he stood in line —but he said he wouldn't miss Callas' *Traviata* if he was down with double pneumonia. And D'Angelo said that personally he could live happily for the rest of his life without hearing Callas butcher *Traviata*

—he was here tonight, he said, only because of the tenor, Richard Tucker."

"That Richard Tucker!" Mom gave her biggest, most motherly smile. "Such a wonderful boy—just as much at home in the *schul* as he is in the opera. What a proud mother he must have!" And Mom gave me a look which made it clear that she still hadn't quite forgiven me for *Rustling Leaves*.

"With such a long standing-room line," I said, "Cohen and D'Angelo had time to whip up a first-class battle. According to Frau Hochschwender—she's a German lady who used to be a concert pianist and now gives piano lessons, and she's also one of the standing-room regulars—Cohen and D'Angelo had never insulted each other so violently in all the years she'd known them. If the box office had opened an hour later, she says they would have come to blows.

"As it turned out, the performance didn't even put an end to their fight. Ordinarily, once the opera began, both men became too wrapped up in the music to remember they were mad at each other—but this time, when the first act ended, Cohen grabbed D'Angelo by the arm and accused him of deliberately groaning after Callas' big aria. 'You did it to ruin the evening for me!' Cohen said. He wouldn't pay attention to D'Angelo's denials. 'I'll get even with you,' he said. 'Wait till the next time Tebaldi is singing!' "

"And the next time Tebaldi was singing," Mom said, "was the night of the murder?"

"Exactly. Three nights ago Tebaldi sang *Tosca*—"

"*Tosca!*" Mom's face lighted up. "Such a beautiful opera! Such a sad story! She's in love with this handsome young artist, and this villain makes advances and tries to force her to give in to him, so she stabs him with a knife. Come to think of it, the villain in that opera is a police officer."

I looked hard, but I couldn't see any trace of sarcasm on Mom's face.

"Those opera plots are really ridiculous, aren't they?" Shirley said. "So exaggerated and unrealistic."

102

"Unrealistic!" Mom turned to her sharply. "You should know some of the things that go on—right here in this building. Didn't Policheck the janitor have his eye on his wife's baby sitter?"

Another fascinating story came out of Mom, and then I went on. "Anyway, for the whole weekend before *Tosca*, D'Angelo worried that Cohen would do something to spoil the performance for him. He worried so much that the night before, he called Cohen up and pleaded with him not to make trouble."

"And Cohen answered?"

"His nephew was in the room with him when the call came. He was going over some account books and didn't really pay attention to what his uncle was saying—but at one point he heard Cohen raise his voice angrily and shout out, 'You can't talk me out of it! When Tebaldi hits her high C in the big aria, I'm going to start booing!' "

Mom shook her head. "Terrible—a terrible threat for a civilized man to make! So does D'Angelo admit that Cohen made it?"

"Well, yes and no. In the early part of the phone conversation, D'Angelo says he and Cohen were yelling at each other so angrily that neither of them listened to what the other one was saying. But later on in the conversation—or so D'Angelo claims—Cohen calmed down and promised to let Tebaldi sing her aria in peace."

"Cohen's nephew says he didn't?"

"Not exactly. He left the room while Cohen was still on the phone—he had to check some receipts in the cash register—so he never heard the end of the conversation. For all he knows Cohen *might* have calmed down and made that promise."

"And what about D'Angelo's end of the phone conversation? Was anybody in the room with him?"

"His wife was. And she swears that he *did* get such a promise out of Cohen. But of course she's his wife, so she's anxious to protect him. And besides she's very deaf, and she won't wear a hearing aid —she's kind of a vain old lady. So what it boils down to, we've got nobody's word except D'Angelo's that Cohen didn't intend to carry out his threat."

"Which brings us," Mom said, "to the night Tebaldi sang *Tosca?*"

MY MOTHER, THE DETECTIVE

"Cohen and D'Angelo both showed up early on the standing-room line that night. Frau Hochschwender says they greeted each other politely, but all the time they were waiting they hardly exchanged a word. No arguments, no differences of opinion—nothing. And her testimony is confirmed by another one of the regulars who was there—Miss Phoebe Van Voorhees. She's an old lady in her seventies, always dresses in black.

"Miss Van Voorhees comes from a wealthy New York family, and when she was a young woman she used to have a regular box at the opera—but the money ran out ten or twelve years ago, and now she lives alone in a cheap hotel in the East Twenties, and she waits on the standing-room line two nights a week. She's so frail-looking you wouldn't think she could stay on her feet for five minutes, much less five hours—but she loves opera, so she does it."

"For love," Mom said, "people can perform miracles."

"Well, Miss Van Voorhees and Frau Hochschwender both say that Cohen and D'Angelo were unusually restrained with each other. Which seems to prove that they were still mad at each other and hadn't made up the quarrel over the phone, as D'Angelo claims—"

"Or maybe it proves the opposite," Mom said. "They did make up the quarrel, and they were so scared of starting another quarrel that they shut up and wouldn't express any opinions."

"Whatever it proves, Mom, here's what happened. On cold nights it's the custom among the standing-room regulars for one of them to go to the cafeteria a block away and get hot coffee for the others—meanwhile they hold his place in the line. The night of Tebaldi's *Tosca* was very cold, and it was D'Angelo's turn to bring the coffee.

"He went for it about forty-five minutes before the box office opened, and got back with it in fifteen or twenty minutes. He was carrying four cardboard containers. Three of them contained coffee with cream and sugar—for Frau Hochschwender, Miss Van Voorhees, and D'Angelo himself. In the fourth container was black coffee without sugar—the way Cohen always took it.

"Well, they all gulped down their coffee, shielding it from the wind with their bodies—and about half an hour later the doors opened. They bought their tickets, went into the opera house and stood together in their usual place in the back, at the center.

"At eight sharp the opera began. Tebaldi was in great voice, and the audience was enthusiastic. At the end of the first act all of the standing-room regulars praised her except Cohen. He just grunted and said nothing. Frau Hochschwender and Miss Van Voorhees both say that he looked pale and a little ill.

" 'Wait till she sings her big aria in the second act,' D'Angelo said. 'I hope she sings it good,' Cohen said—and Frau Hochschwender says there was a definite threat in his voice. But Miss Van Voorhees says she didn't notice anything significant in his voice—to her it just sounded like an offhand remark. Then the second act began, and it was almost time for Tebaldi's big aria—"

"Such a beautiful aria!" Mom said. "*Vissy darty*. It's Italian. She's telling that police officer villain that all her life she's cared only for love and for art, and she never wanted to hurt a soul. She tells him this, and a little later she stabs him." And in a low voice, a little quavery but really kind of pretty, Mom began to half sing and half hum—"*Vissy darty, vissy damory*"— Then she broke off, and did something I had seldom seen her do. She blushed.

There was a moment of silence, while Shirley and I carefully refrained from looking at each other. Then I said, "So a few minutes before Tebaldi's big aria, Cohen suddenly gave a groan, then he grabbed hold of Frau Hochschwender's arm and said, 'I'm sick—' And then he started making strangling noises, and dropped like a lead weight to the floor.

"Somebody went for a doctor, and D'Angelo got down on his knees by Cohen and said, 'Cohen, Cohen, what's the matter?' And Cohen, with his eyes straight on D'Angelo's face, said, 'You no-good! You deserve to die for what you did!' Those were his exact words, Mom—half a dozen people heard them.

"Then a doctor came, with a couple of ushers, and they took Cohen out to the lobby—and D'Angelo, Frau Hochschwender, and Miss Van Voorhees followed. A little later an ambulance came, but Cohen was dead before he got to the hospital.

MY MOTHER, THE DETECTIVE

"At first the doctors thought it was a heart attack, but they did a routine autopsy—and found enough poison in his stomach to kill a man half his age and twice his strength. The dose he swallowed must've taken two to three hours to produce a reaction—which means he swallowed it while he was on the standing-room line. Well, nobody saw him swallow *anything* on the standing-room line except that container of hot black coffee."

"And when the doctors looked at the contents of his stomach?"

"They found the traces of his lunch, which *couldn't* have contained the poison or he would've died long before he got to the opera house—and they found that coffee—and that was all they found. So the coffee had to be what killed him."

"And since that old man D'Angelo was the one who gave him the coffee, you naturally think he's the murderer."

"What else can we think, Mom? For five minutes or so—from the time he picked up the coffee at the cafeteria to the time he gave it to Cohen at the opera house D'Angelo was alone with it. Nobody was watching him—he could easily have slipped something into it. And nobody *else* had such an opportunity. Cohen took the coffee from D'Angelo, turned away to shield the container from the cold wind, and drank it all down then and there. Only D'Angelo *could* have put the poison into it."

"What about the man at the cafeteria who made the coffee?"

"That doesn't make sense, Mom. The man at the cafeteria would have no way of knowing who the coffee was meant for. He'd have to be a complete psycho who didn't care who he poisoned. Just the same, though, we checked him out. He poured the coffee into the container directly from a big urn—twenty other people had been drinking coffee from that same urn. Then in front of a dozen witnesses he handed the container to D'Angelo without putting a thing in it—not even sugar, because Cohen never took his coffee with sugar. So we're right back to D'Angelo—he *has* to be the murderer."

"And where did he get it, this deadly poison? Correct me if I'm wrong but such an item isn't something you can pick up at your local supermarket."

106

"Sure, it's against the law to sell poison to the general public. But you'd be surprised how easy it is to get hold of the stuff anyway. The kind that killed Cohen is a common commercial compound—it's used to mix paints, for metallurgy, in certain medicines, in insecticides. Ordinary little pellets of rat poison are made of it sometimes, and you can buy them at your local hardware store—a couple of dozen kids swallow them by accident in this city every year. And don't forget, D'Angelo used to be in the exterminating business—he knows all the sources, it would be easier for him to get his hands on poison than for most other people."

"So you've arrested him for the murder?" Mom said.

I gave a sigh. "No, we haven't."

"How come? What's holding you up?"

"It's the motive, Mom. D'Angelo and Cohen had absolutely no connection with each other outside of the standing-room line. Cohen didn't leave D'Angelo any money, he wasn't having an affair with D'Angelo's wife, he didn't know a deep dark secret out of D'Angelo's past. There's only one reason why D'Angelo could have killed him— to stop him from booing at the end of Renata Tebaldi's big aria. That's why he committed the murder. I'm morally certain of it, and so is everyone else in the Department. And so is the D.A.'s office— but they won't let us make the arrest."

"And why not?"

"Because nobody believes for one moment that we can get a jury to believe such a motive. Juries are made up of ordinary everyday people. They don't go to the opera. They think it's all a lot of nonsense—fat women screaming at fat men, in a foreign language. I can sympathize with them—I think so myself. Can you imagine the D.A. standing up in front of a jury and saying, 'The defendant was so crazy about an opera singer's voice that he killed a man for disagreeing with him!' The jury would laugh in the D.A.'s face."

I sighed harder than before. "We've got an airtight case. The perfect opportunity. No other possible suspects. The dying man's accusation—'You no-good! You deserve to die for what you did!' But we don't dare bring the killer to trial."

MY MOTHER, THE DETECTIVE

Mom didn't say anything for a few seconds. Her eyes were almost shut, the corners of her mouth were turned down. I know this expression well—her "thinking" expression. Something always comes out of it.

Finally she looked up and gave a nod. "Thank God for juries!"

"What do you mean, Mom?"

"I mean, if it wasn't for ordinary everyday people with common sense, God knows *who* you experts would be sending to jail!"

"Mom, are you saying that D'Angelo *didn't*—"

"I'm saying nothing. Not yet. First I'm asking. Four questions."

No doubt about it, whenever Mom starts asking her questions, that means she's on the scent, she's getting ready to hand me a solution to another one of my cases.

My feelings, as always, were mixed. On the one hand, nobody admires Mom more than I do—her deep knowledge of human nature acquired among her friends and neighbors in the Bronx, her uncanny sharpness in applying that knowledge to the crimes I tell her about from time to time.

On the other hand—well, how ecstatic is a man supposed to get at the idea that his mother can do his own job better than *he* can? That's why I've never been able to talk about Mom's talent to anybody else in the Department—except, of course, to Inspector Millner, my immediate superior, and only because he's a bachelor, and Shirley and I are trying to get something going between Mom and him.

So I guess my voice wasn't as enthusiastic as it should have been, when I said to Mom, "Okay, what are your four questions?"

"First I bring in the peach pie," Mom said.

We waited while the dishes were cleared, and new dishes were brought. Then the heavenly aroma of Mom's peach pie filled the room. One taste of it, and my enthusiasm began to revive. "What *are* your questions, Mom?"

She lifted her finger. "Number One: you mentioned that Cohen had a cold a week ago, the night Maria Callas was singing *Traviata*. Did he still have the same cold three nights ago, when Tebaldi was singing *Tosca*?"

MOM SINGS AN ARIA

By this time I ought to be used to Mom's questions. I ought to take it on faith that they are not as irrelevant as they sound. But I still can't quite keep the bewilderment out of my voice.

"As a matter of fact," I said, "Cohen *did* have a cold the night of the murder. Frau Hochschwender and Miss Van Voorhees both mentioned it—he was sneezing while he waited in line, and even a few times during the performance, though he tried hard to control himself."

Mom's face gave no indication whether this was or wasn't what she had wanted to hear. She lifted another finger. "Number Two: after the opera every night, was it the custom for those standing-room regulars to separate right away—or did they maybe stay together, for a little while before they finally said good night?"

"They usually went to the cafeteria a block away—the same place where D'Angelo bought the coffee that Cohen drank—and sat at a table for an hour or so and discussed the performance they'd just heard. Over coffee and doughnuts—or Danish pastry."

Mom gave a nod, and lifted another finger. "Number Three: at the hospital you naturally examined what was in Cohen's pockets? Did you find something like an envelope—a small envelope with absolutely nothing in it?"

That question really made me jump. "We did find an envelope, Mom! Ordinary stationery size—it was unsealed, and there was no address or stamp on it. But how in the world did you—"

Mom's fourth finger was in the air. "Number Four: how many more times this season is Renata Tebaldi supposed to sing *Tosca?*"

"It was Tebaldi's first, last, and only performance of *Tosca* this season," I said. "The posters in front of the opera house said so. But I don't see what that has to do with—"

"You don't see," Mom said. "Naturally. You're like all the younger generation these days. So scientific. Facts you see. D'Angelo was the only one who was ever alone with Cohen's coffee —so D'Angelo must have put the poison in. A fact, so you see it. But what about the *people* already? Who is D'Angelo—who was Cohen —what type human beings? This you wouldn't ask yourself. Probably you wouldn't even understand about my Uncle Julius and the World Series."

"I'm sorry, Mom. I never knew you *had* an Uncle Julius—"

"I don't have him no more. That's the point of the story. All his life he was a fan from the New York Yankees. He rooted for them, he bet money on them, and when they played the World Series he was always there to watch them. Until a couple of years ago when he had his heart attack, and he was in the hospital at World Series time.

" 'I'll watch the New York Yankees on television,' he said. 'The excitement is too much for you,' the doctor said, 'it'll kill you.' But Uncle Julius had his way, and he watched the World Series. Every day he watched, and every night the doctor said, 'You'll be dead before morning.' And Uncle said, 'I wouldn't die till I know how the World Series comes out!' So finally the New York Yankees won the World Series—and an hour later Uncle Julius went to sleep and died."

Mom stopped talking, and looked around at Shirley and me. Then she shook her head and said, "You don't follow yet? A man with a love for something that's outside himself, that isn't even his family—a love for the New York Yankees or for Renata Tebaldi—in such a man this feeling is stronger than his personal worries or his personal ambitions. He wouldn't let anything interrupt his World Series in the middle, not even dying. He wouldn't let anything interrupt his opera in the middle—not even murdering."

I began to see a glimmer of Mom's meaning. "You're talking about D'Angelo, Mom?"

"Who else? Renata Tebaldi was singing her one and only *Tosca* for the year, and for D'Angelo, Renata Tebaldi is the greatest singer alive. Never—in a million years, never—would he do anything to spoil this performance for himself, to make him walk out of it before the end. Let's say he *did* want to murder Cohen. The last time in the world he'd pick for this murder would be in the middle of Tebaldi's *Tosca*—her one and only *Tosca*! Especially since he could wait just as easy till after the opera, when the standing-room regulars would be having cake and coffee at the cafeteria—he could just as easy poison Cohen then."

110

"But Mom, isn't that kind of far-fetched, psychologically? If the average man was worked up enough to commit a murder, he wouldn't care about hearing the end of an opera first!"

"Excuse me, Davie—the average man's psychology we're not talking about. The opera lover's psychology we are talking about. This is why you and the Homicide Squad and the District Attorney couldn't make heads and tails from this case. Because you don't understand from opera lovers. In this world they don't live—they've got a world of their own. Inside their heads things are going on which other people's heads never even dreamed about. To solve this case you have to think like an opera lover."

"To solve this case, Mom, you have to answer the basic question: if D'Angelo didn't poison that coffee, who *could* have?"

"Who says the coffee was poisoned?"

"But I told you about the autopsy. The poison took two to three hours to work, and the contents of Cohen's stomach—"

"The contents of his stomach! You should show a little more interest in the contents of Cohen's pockets!"

"There was nothing unusual in his pockets—"

"Why should a man carry in his pocket an empty unsealed envelope, without any writing on it, without even a stamp on it? Only because it wasn't empty when he put it there. Something was in it—something which he expected to need later on in the evening—something which he finally took out of the envelope—"

"What are you talking about, Mom?"

"I'm talking about Cohen's cold. An ordinary man, he don't think twice about going to the opera with a cold. What's the difference if he sneezes a little? It's only music. But to an opera lover, sneezing during a performance, disturbing people, competing with the singers—this is worse than a major crime. A real opera lover like Cohen, he'd do everything he could to keep his cold under control.

"Which explains what he put in that envelope before he left his home to go to the opera house. A pill, what else? One of these new prescription cold pills that dries up your nose and keeps you from sneezing for five-six hours. And why was the envelope empty when you found it in his pocket? Because half an hour before the box office opened, he slipped out his pill and swallowed it down with his hot black coffee."

"Nobody *saw* him taking that pill, Mom."

"Why should anybody see him? Like you explained yourself, to drink his coffee he had to turn his body away and shield the container from the wind."

I was beginning to be shaken, no doubt about it. But Shirley spoke up now, in her sweet voice, the voice she always uses when she thinks she's one up on Mom. "The facts don't seem to bear you out, Mother. All the witnesses say that Mr. Cohen went on sneezing *after* the opera had begun. Well, if he really did take a cold pill, as you believe, why didn't it have any effect on his symptoms?"

A gleam came to Mom's eyes, and I could see she was about to pounce. The fact is that Shirley never learns.

So to spare my wife's feelings I broke in quickly, before Mom could open her mouth. "I'm afraid that confirms Mom's theory, honey. The reason why the cold pill didn't work was that it wasn't a cold pill. It looked like one on the outside maybe, but it actually contained poison."

"I always knew I didn't produce a dope!" Mom said, with a big satisfied smile. "So now the answer is simple, no? If Cohen was carrying around a poison pill in his pocket, where did he get it? Who gave it to him? Why, should he think it was a cold pill? Because somebody told him it was. Somebody he thought he could trust— not only personally but professionally. Somebody he went to and said, 'Give me some of that new stuff, that new wonder drug, that'll keep me from sneezing during the opera—' "

"His nephew!" I interrupted. "My God, Mom, I think you're right. Cohen's nephew *is* a pharmacist—he manages the drug store that Cohen owned. He has access to all kinds of poison and he could make up a pill that would look like a real cold pill. And what's more, he's the only relative Cohen has in the world. He inherits Cohen's store and Cohen's savings."

Mom spread her hands. "So there you are. You couldn't ask for a more ordinary, old-fashioned motive for murder. Any jury will be able to understand it. It isn't one bit operatic."

"But Mom, you must've suspected Cohen's nephew from the start. Otherwise you wouldn't have asked your question about the empty envelope."

"Naturally I suspected him. It was the lie he told."

"What lie?"

"The night before the opera D'Angelo called up Cohen and tried to make up their quarrel. Now according to the nephew, Cohen made a threat to D'Angelo over the phone. 'When Tebaldi hits her high C in the big aria, I'm going to start booing!' A terrible threat—but Cohen never could have made it."

"I don't see why not—"

"Because Cohen was an opera lover, that's why. A high C—this is a tenor's note. It's the top of his range—when he hits one, everybody is thrilled and says how wonderful he is. But for a soprano a high C is nothing special. She can go a lot higher than that. A high E—sometimes even an E sharp—*this* is the big note for a soprano. In the *Vissy darty* from *Tosca*, any soprano who couldn't do better than a high C world be strictly an amateur. People who are ignoramuses about opera—people like Cohen's nephew—they never *heard* of anything except the high C. But an opera lover like Cohen—he positively couldn't make such a mistake. Now excuse me, I'll bring in the coffee."

Mom got to her feet, and then Shirley called out, "Wait a second, Mother. If his nephew committed the murder, why did Cohen accuse D'Angelo of doing it?"

"When did Cohen accuse D'Angelo?"

"His dying words. He looked into D'Angelo's face and said, "You no-good! You deserve to die for what you did!""

"He looked into D'Angelo's face—but how do you know it was D'Angelo he was seeing? He was in delirium from the weakness and the pain, and before his eyes he wasn't seeing any D'Angelo, he wasn't seeing this world that the rest of us are living in. He was seeing the world he'd been looking at before he got sick, the world that meant the most to him—he was seeing the world of the opera, what else? And what was happening up there on that stage just before the poison hit him? The no-good villain was making advances to the beautiful heroine, and she was struggling to defend herself, and pretty soon she was going to kill him—and Cohen, seeing that villain in front of his eyes, shouted out at him, 'You no-good! You deserve to die for what you did!' "

Mom was silent for a moment, and then she went on in a lower voice, "An opera lover will go on being an opera lover—right up to the end."

She went out to the kitchen for the coffee, and I went to the phone in the hall to call the Homicide Squad.

When I got back to the table Mom was seated and the coffee was served. She took a few sips, and then gave a little sigh. "Poor old Cohen—such a terrible way to go!"

"Death by poisoning *is* pretty painful," I said.

"Poisoning?" Mom blinked up at me. "Yes, this is terrible too. But the worst part of all—the poor man died fifteen minutes too soon. He never heard Tebaldi sing *Vissy darty*."

And Mom began to hum softly.

MOM AND THE HAUNTED MINK

"IT'S MY PERSONAL OPINION," MOM SAID, "THAT mink is overrated. I've been wearing it for years, and believe me—"

"With all respect, Mother," said my wife Shirley, "I've been in this family over seven years, and I can't remember *ever* seeing you in mink. In fact, you don't even own—"

"All right, I wouldn't argue with you," Mom said. "If you say I never wore mink—if you say I'm getting *meshuganer* in my old age—it must be the truth. After all, which one of us graduated from Wellesley College?" Then Mom took another sip of noodle soup, and sighed, "It isn't as good as what I make at home."

It was a very unusual Friday night. Mom's kitchen stove was being fixed, so she couldn't give Shirley and me dinner up in the Bronx. Instead we were taking *her* to dinner at Fingerhood's, the fancy kosher restaurant near Times Square.

The crowd here was a mixture of sharp Broadway and elderly middle-class. Mom studied her fellow diners with the same penetrating, positively dissecting gaze that she gave to butchers while they weighed her meat. It was the couple in the corner—a little bald-headed man in his fifties and a tall blonde in her twenties, buried in furs—who caused Mom to make her remark about mink.

And of course Shirley couldn't leave the remark unchallenged. After seven years of challenging Mom, Shirley still won't admit that she's outclassed. And so—though *I* couldn't remember Mom ever wearing mink either—I quickly changed the subject. "Talking about mink," I said, "we got a crazy murder case over the weekend."

Mom's eyes lighted up. Nothing makes her forget small injuries faster than a chance to hear about one of my cases at the Homicide Squad. "So maybe you'll tell me about it?" she said.

MY MOTHER, THE DETECTIVE

I started right in. "This Mrs. Laura McCloskey is the wife of Dr. Alfred McCloskey—he's an old-fashioned G.P., one of the vanishing breed. For years he and his wife have lived on the West Side in a three-story brownstone which he bought back in the thirties. The top two floors are their home, and the ground floor is his office. The neighborhood isn't what it used to be, but I guess he doesn't want to sell the house and move elsewhere. He makes a fairly comfortable living, but nothing spectacular. That's why he never bought his wife a mink coat until recently."

"She's been wanting one for a long time?" Mom said.

"For twenty-five years, since they got married, according to Dr. McCloskey. She hasn't exactly nagged him about it—he was very careful to explain that—but he could tell how she felt every time they passed a mink coat on the street or every time she mentioned one of her friends' mink coats. Well, I never knew a woman yet who couldn't get her wishes across without coming right out and expressing them."

"It's strictly self-defense," Mom said. "I never knew a man who wouldn't automatically say no if a woman asked him for something right out."

"Anyway, Mom, a couple of months ago Mrs. McCloskey had a birthday, and the doctor gave her a mink coat. For years he'd been saving for this, and he took out a bank loan for the difference, but he still couldn't have managed it without getting an unexpected break. One of his patients told him about Madame Rosa, a wholesale fur dealer who sometimes has unusual bargains to offer. Dr. McCloskey went down to Madame Rosa's place and bought a mink coat that had just come in. It wasn't cheap—he paid close to five thousand dollars for it, but it would've cost three times as much at any retail store."

"Strictly a legal transaction, I hope?"

"The coat wasn't hot, if that's what you mean. Dr. McCloskey found out its whole history from the wholesaler."

"That's Madame Rosa?"

"Actually it's a man named Harry Schultz, who lives in Englewood, New Jersey. He uses the trade name Madame Rosa, in honor of a fortune-teller in Atlantic City years ago who advised him to go into the fur business. Well, he explained to Dr. McCloskey that the mink coat was part of the estate of Oscar F. Tannenbaum, a stock broker who died a little while ago. This coat was the last thing Tannenbaum ever gave to his wife, Janet—then his investments failed, he lost all his money, and he jumped off the terrace of his Park Avenue apartment.

"Mrs. Tannenbaum was forced to sell all her possessions to pay off her husband's debts. There was a public auction, and she sat in the back of the room. When the mink coat came up for sale, she lost control of herself and started bidding on it herself. She didn't have a dime, you understand, but the auctioneer just couldn't make her stop bidding. When the coat was finally bought by Madame Rosa— that is, by Harry Schultz—Mrs. Tannenbaum screamed at him that he had no right to it, it was hers, and she'd never let any other woman wear it. Then she collapsed—some kind of stroke—and the next day she was dead.

"And that's the coat's history, as reported by Harry Schultz. We've checked it out, and it seems to be accurate. The auction house, incidentally, valued the coat at fifteen thousand dollars, though they're not obliged to tell us what Harry Schultz actually paid for it."

"And Mrs. McCloskey was happy with her mink?" Mom said.

"At first the doctor was afraid she wouldn't be, because he had picked it out himself, without consulting her. But he wanted the gift to be a surprise—and luckily she loved it. It made her as happy as a girl. First she hugged him and kissed him, then she burst into tears, then she put on the coat and posed in front of her mirror for an hour. And that night she made him take her out to a restaurant so she could show off the coat—even though it was too warm for furs."

"So much emphasis on material possessions!" Shirley said. "No wonder this story has a tragic ending."

Mom turned to Shirley. "If Davie offered you such a material possession right now, you wouldn't take the risk?"

I broke in quickly, before Shirley could commit herself. "Dr. McCloskey told his wife the coat's history—all about the auction and Mrs. Tannenbaum's outburst—and his wife made a funny remark.

MY MOTHER, THE DETECTIVE

'I do hope the poor woman wasn't serious about her threat,' she said. 'I hope she doesn't decide to come back from the grave—' She laughed, although Dr. McCloskey could see that a tiny part of her wasn't really joking.

"But he didn't think twice about it. His wife was the kind of person who goes to seances, follows every horoscope in the daily paper, believes in mind reading and crystal balls and so on. After twenty-five years of marriage Dr. McCloskey didn't pay much attention to her superstitions."

The waiter came to take away our soup bowls and bring our main courses, so I had to stop my story. The waiters at Fingerhood's are the most accomplished story-killers in New York.

The waiter went away, and I started in again. "A couple of weeks later a funny incident took place. Mrs. McCloskey and the doctor were about to leave the house for a dinner date. She asked her maid —that's Berenice Webley, a colored girl in her late twenties—to fetch the coat for her. The maid went to the bedroom closet, and a moment later she called out, 'I just can't seem to get this coat off the hanger!'

"Mrs. McCloskey went to the closet too, and tugged at the coat, fast. 'It's as if something was *holding* it on there,' she said. Finally Dr. McCloskey gave a hard pull and the coat came off. 'The hanger must've got caught in one of the sleeves,' he said—though he says now that he wasn't really so sure; when he yanked at that coat, it actually did feel as if some force were yanking back. Then his wife said, 'Well, as long as it isn't that Mrs. Tannenbaum carrying out her threat—' But she was too embarrassed to finish her sentence."

"And well she might be," Shirley said. "A dead woman haunting a mink coat! I've never heard of anything so absurd!"

"Dead women can act very much alive sometimes," Mom said. "My nephew Jonathan is still a bachelor, because his mother don't approve of modern girls—and his mother's been dead for eighteen years."

"A week later," I went on, "there was another funny incident. Mrs. McCloskey belonged to a literary club—a group of middle-aged women who meet every Thursday at one another's homes and discuss

118

the latest best-selling books. Most of the ladies have more money than Mrs. McCloskey—their husbands are successful businessmen or professional men who aren't quite as idealistic as the doctor. For years Mrs. McCloskey was one of the few members of the club who never wore a mink coat to any of the meetings. So naturally, now that she finally owned one, she had to show it off on Thursday afternoon.

"The meeting was held out in Scarsdale, at the home of Mrs. Alonzo Martineau—her husband is a big surgeon with a Park Avenue office. There was always a kind of feud between Mrs. McCloskey and Mrs. Martineau, probably because both husbands are medical men. The first time she saw the mink, Mrs. Martineau made a remark about how pleased she was that Dr. McCloskey's practice was doing so well these days—and Mrs. McCloskey answered that her husband's practice had always done well, only she didn't believe in boasting about such things the way *some* people do.

"Well, a few hours later the meeting broke up, and the ladies left the house and started down the front walk to their cars. Mrs. McCloskey came a little behind the others, in order to be next to her friend Mrs. Harmon, the banker's wife, who was going to give her a ride home. Mrs. Harmon is an elderly lady, and couldn't move as fast as the others.

"Suddenly, halfway down the walk, Mrs. McCloskey gave a yell and grabbed at her neck. As she described it to her husband that night, her mink coat seemed to jump right off her shoulders of its own accord—it landed on the lawn, and started sliding across the grass."

"What kind of drinks do they serve at these literary meetings?" Shirley said.

"Old Mrs. Harmon never takes anything stronger than tea—and she saw the coat go sailing through the air too, and she saw Mrs. McCloskey run after it and scoop it up from the grass. The other ladies didn't turn around soon enough to see the flying coat, so Mrs. McCloskey laughed and told them she had tripped and the coat had fallen off her back. Mrs. Martineau made a crack about people who are so rich they can afford to throw away their minks, and the incident passed off as a joke.

"But Mrs. McCloskey was terribly upset about it. 'There's something *wrong* with this coat,' she kept saying to her husband that night, 'I can feel the *presence* of something—some kind of evil spirit!' And no matter how hard he tried, Dr. McCloskey couldn't calm her down and convince her she was just imagining things."

"But the incident on the lawn was an obvious hallucination," Shirley said. "Subconsciously Mrs. McCloskey rejected and despised the materialistic side of her nature as symbolized by the mink coat. And so, with no voluntary effort or even conscious awareness, she flung it off her back onto Mrs. Martineau's lawn."

"And the old lady, Mrs. Harmon?" Mom said. "She had a hallucination too?"

"There *is* such a thing as mass hypnosis," Shirley said.

"Maybe so," I said, "but there were half a dozen more incidents in the next two weeks, all of which Mrs. McCloskey reported to her husband. She'd try to throw her coat over her chair in a restaurant, and it would keep slipping to the floor. She'd be walking along the street, and suddenly the coat would seem to be pushing against her, trying to move her in the opposite direction. One afternoon, right after she hung it up in her bedroom closet, she thought she heard it thumping against the inside of the closet door. And finally the most frightening incident of all—"

"How's the pot-roast—all right?" said the waiter.

"Personally I like to use more paprika," Mom said, "but otherwise it isn't the worst I ever tasted."

The waiter shrugged and moved away, and Mom turned back to me. "So? The most frightening incident of all?"

"At two o'clock in the morning," I said, "Dr. McCloskey was awakened by his wife. She was scared to death, he says, and on the verge of hysterics. 'It's getting away, it's getting away!' she kept screaming. 'It slid across the floor, it went out to the foyer!'

"Dr. McCloskey saw that the door to the bedroom closet was wide open, and the bedroom door was open too. So he got out of bed and went to the foyer—and believe it or not, he saw the mink coat wrapped around the handle of the front door. The foyer light was dim, and the doctor was still half asleep, but he swears that it looked for one moment as if that mink coat were trying to turn the handle of the door—as if it wanted to get out to the stairs and go down to the ground floor and leave the house!

"Well, he grabbed hold of the coat and pulled it off the door handle, and then he told himself that he was developing as big an imagination as his wife."

"Does he think it was his imagination that got the coat from the bedroom closet to the front door?" Mom said.

"He thinks it never *was* in the bedroom closet. His wife and he came in late from a party that night—she was exhausted, a little groggy, and the house was overheated. He thinks she took off her coat the moment she stepped inside and hung it on the door handle without realizing what she was doing, and then went straight to bed. As for seeing the coat slide across the room—well, he thinks she dreamed that, one of those terribly vivid dreams, that seem to be real even after you wake up."

Mom gave a snort. "A woman who's dying to have a mink coat all her life—she hangs it up at night on a door handle?"

"What other explanation is there?" I said. "Anyway, Mrs. McCloskey couldn't get to sleep the rest of that night, even though her husband put the coat in the closet and locked the closet door. And the next day she made up her mind to find out the truth once and for all—was the coat haunted by the ghost of Mrs. Tannenbaum, or wasn't it?"

"How on earth *could* she find out such a thing?" Shirley said.

"By asking Mrs. Tannenbaum direct, how else?" Mom said. "Am I right, Davie?"

"Absolutely. Mrs. McCloskey believed in seances, as I told you. She had a favorite spiritualist—a Mrs. Vivian who lives in a small apartment on a rundown genteel street in the Village. She's a widow in her fifties—a wispy, gray-haired little woman. For the last ten years, since her husband died, she's been trying to earn a living as a medium and astrologist. The bunco squad knows all about her, but it's never been worthwhile to pull her in. She only operates in a small way—five or ten bucks per customer—and hardly makes enough to pay her monthly rent. What's more, she seems to believe in her own spiritualistic powers. When the dead speak through her mouth, she's just as impressed as any one of her clients.

"So Mrs. McCloskey took her mink coat down to Mrs. Vivian. And she didn't go by herself—she took her friend, old Mrs. Harmon of the literary club, along. 'Whatever happens,' she said, 'I want to be sure it isn't only in my imagination.' Well, Mrs. Vivian put the mink on the table in front of her, turned out the lights, and went into her trance—clasping her hands, rolling her eyes, moaning and groaning. And pretty soon a voice came out of her, much deeper and more belligerent than her own natural voice. 'This is Juliet Tannenbaum talking,' it said. 'How dare you wear the coat that belongs to me! You'd better get rid of it, or I'll never give you any peace! Do what I say, or I'll drive you into an early grave!'

"That was Mrs. Tannenbaum's message—old Mrs. Harmon remembers it word for word. Mrs. McCloskey repeated it later to her husband, and Mrs. Vivian told us about it when we questioned her."

"Mrs. Vivian can hear what she says in her trances?"

"She's wide-awake at all times, Mom. The voice coming out of her, she says, seems to belong to somebody else. She has no idea what it's going to say—she listens to it just as curiously as her clients do.

"Well, after she left Mrs. Vivian's place, Mrs. McCloskey went straight to her husband's office. She told him she wanted to get rid of the coat. It broke her heart to do it, because it was so beautiful, but she was too frightened to keep it. What's more, the experience had upset her so much that she didn't even want another mink coat in its place.

"When the coat was sold, she said, he could keep the money—she had learned her lesson and she was through with expensive luxuries for good. The doctor tried to talk her out of this, but she wouldn't change her mind. Then she left him and went off to her Wednesday afternoon Philharmonic concert, where the coat appeared in public for the last time."

"And the doctor sold the coat?" Mom said.

"After his wife left, he called up Harry Schultz—that is, Madame Rosa—and asked for the name of the auction house which had auctioned off the coat in the first place. Schultz offered to buy the coat back for what the doctor had paid for it, but the doctor decided to take his chances with an auction. He called the auction house and arranged for them to pick up the coat the next day. But they never did."

Mom leaned forward, holding her fork in the air, completely forgetting to plunge it into her baked potato. The fact is, she smelled blood. Nobody on earth has a kinder heart than Mom—when I was a kid, she could never bring herself to spank me; but she *does* enjoy a good murder story.

"The doctor and his wife stayed home that night and watched television," I said. "But around eleven he got an emergency call from a patient in Brooklyn. So he got in his car and drove away, leaving his wife alone in the house."

"The maid don't sleep in?" Mom said.

"Berenice Webley? She comes in early every morning to make breakfast—she's got her own key—and leaves every night after dinner. Well, when the doctor got to Brooklyn he found it wasn't his patient who had called him—it was some kind of practical joke. He was mad as a wet hen, and he drove home again. He was gone nearly two hours. When he got back to his front door, he found it unlocked. This worried him, because he had distinctly heard his wife snap the bolt behind him.

"The doctor stepped inside and called out to her. No answer. He went upstairs and found her in the bedroom, sprawled on the bed. Her dress was torn, and the bedspread was rumpled. She was dead —she had died thirty to sixty minutes earlier. At first Dr. McCloskey thought she might've had a heart attack, but later the autopsy showed she had been smothered to death. Some large thick soft object had been held tightly over her face—or maybe I should say that it held *itself* over her face."

"Meaning?" Mom pushed her chin forward.

"Small bits of fur were found on her lips and in her nostrils. Mink fur, Mom. As for the mink coat—well, its box, with Madame Rosa's label on it, was lying empty on the floor, as if Mrs. McCloskey had been in the act of packing it up. But the mink coat itself was gone."

I stopped talking. Let's face it, I was kind of pleased with the effect I had made.

Finally Shirley spoke up. "For heaven's sake, David, does the New York Homicide Squad—grown men, living in the twentieth century!—actually believe that this woman was smothered by a haunted coat?"

"Officially," I said, "the New York Homicide Squad only believes in flesh-and-blood killers. That's what we're looking for in this case. But so far we can't find anybody, outside of that ghost, who has a motive. Mrs. McCloskey was a harmless little woman without an enemy in the world. Her marriage was happy, and her husband hasn't been playing around on the side—and don't think we haven't dug into his private life! All their financial assets, including the house, are in his name—he doesn't inherit a thing by her death, not even any insurance. They've got one son—he's married, practices medicine in Michigan, and hasn't quarreled with his parents. Anyway, he was home in bed on the night of the murder."

"And how about robbery?" Mom said. "A valuable item *is* missing, no?"

"It had to be a very peculiar robber who took that coat. Mrs. McCloskey had a box full of jewelry on top of her dresser—and not one piece was missing. On the bed table was the doctor's billfold, with almost two hundred dollars in small bills inside of it, and the contents were intact."

"Two hundred dollars! What was he doing with so much cash?"

"His hobby is collecting books—first editions and so on. Well, the afternoon of the murder he sold a few of his books to a dealer. He got paid in cash, and he had to take the money home with him because the banks were already closed.

"But there's another reason why it probably wasn't a robber who killed her. As soon as the doctor left the house at eleven that night, his wife bolted the front door. He swears he heard her do it—she always *did* do it when she had to be alone in the house at night. But when he got home nearly two hours later, the door was unlocked and unbolted—and no sign that it had been forced, no sign that any of the windows had been forced."

MOM AND THE HAUNTED MINK

"So it must have been Mrs. McCloskey herself who opened the door to the killer. But she was a nervous woman. She never would've let in a stranger—only somebody she knew."

"Didn't you say her maid had an extra key to the house?" Shirley said.

"The maid, Berenice Webley, has an airtight alibi. She was at a dance up at 125th Street—in full view of a hundred people until after two o'clock in the morning. Besides, her key couldn't have been any use for opening the bolt. So there you are. The killer wasn't a robber, and nobody who knew the woman has the slightest motive. Who's left? Only Mrs. Tannenbaum's ghost."

"Excuse me," Mom said, "but the ghost didn't have a motive either. The ghost told Mrs. McCloskey she should get rid of that mink coat or else she'd end up in an early grave. So Mrs. McCloskey *listened* to the warning, didn't she? She *was* getting rid of the coat. So why did the ghost have to kill her?"

I suddenly felt very tired. For three days the boys down at Homicide—the ones who weren't working on this case—had been making jokes about ghosts. The subject of ghosts was beginning to lose its charm for me.

"I don't know, Mom," I said. "Is there a rule that a ghost has to have a sense of fairplay? Maybe this ghost *enjoys* killing people. Or maybe it didn't believe that Mrs. McCloskey really wanted to get rid of the coat. Or maybe—"

But Mom was frowning—that dark frown which shows she's got an idea percolating. "The ghost didn't believe—she didn't really want—" Mom began to nod her head, and then she looked up at me, and there was a big smile on her face. "It's possible, Davie! It's a definite possibility! Thank you kindly for the suggestion!"

"What suggestion, Mom? If you're on to something—"

"On to something? How could this be? A little *nebbish* like me, who don't even know what kind of a coat she wears? But maybe I *could* be on to something—if I heard the answers to three or four questions."

I shot a warning glance at Shirley, then I said, "I'll tell you whatever I can, Mom."

MY MOTHER, THE DETECTIVE

"First call the waiter and order me some of the apple strudel."

I motioned to the waiter, we ordered our desserts, and then Mom raised her finger. "Question Number One. Was Dr. McCloskey selling a lot of his books lately?"

"As a matter of fact, he was—a dozen or more in the last three weeks. Also he was economizing on cigars and steam baths and so on. He figured he had to, if he ever expected to pay off the money the bank had loaned him to buy that mink coat."

Mom gave one of her nods—carefully not letting me know if she was happy with the answer or not. "Question Number Two. The old lady Mrs. Harmon—the one that went to the seance with the doctor's wife—just exactly how near-sighted is she?"

"I'm sorry, Mom, but that's a bad guess. She isn't near-sighted at all. As a matter of fact, Mrs, Harmon is terribly far-sighted. She has to wear glasses for reading, but not for walking along the street."

"She isn't near-sighted? You're positive of this? All right—so, Question Number Three. This woman with the seances, this Mrs. Vivian, has she maybe been a little richer lately than she usually is?"

No doubt of it, this question pulled me up short. "I don't know how you knew that, Mom, but she *has* been. We keep a routine check on people connected with murder cases, and the other day our man reported that Mrs. Vivian went to Macy's and paid a lot of money—in cash—for a new living-room sofa. We asked her where she got the money—since she's usually so strapped—and she told us she'd been saving it for years in a box in her closet. Well, we can't *prove* she's lying—but our guess is she's latched on to some gullible female who has more to spend than most of her other clients."

Mom nodded. "So—Question Number Four. The doctor's wife —was she the type person who had trouble remembering people's names?"

"Mom, what kind of question—"

"Am I asking, or am I answering?"

"Okay, okay. Well, actually Mrs. McCloskey was that type— vague and forgetful, that is. Her husband told us how she embarrassed him sometimes by calling their oldest friends by the wrong names. He didn't say it about her reproachfully, though—it seemed to be one of the reasons why he loved her."

"Exactly," Mom said. "He loved her, and she loved him . . . That's the whole point about this case. That's the explanation for the ghost. Good—here's our strudel."

And Mom wouldn't say another word about the murder until she had tasted the strudel, frowned a little, then announced that it needed more cinnamon.

"You were saying, Mom? The explanation for the ghost?"

Mom gave a little smile. "Did I ever tell you about your Aunt Doris that everybody said was the dumbest woman in the United States of America?"

"I never knew I *had* an Aunt Doris."

"She's dead now, poor thing. She married your Papa's oldest brother, Saul. They moved out to Hollywood, California, and he got to be a big shot in the movie business. Such a brilliant man. He read books—long heavy ones, by Russian writers. And he listened to symphony music—he didn't just go to the concerts and fall asleep, he actually listened. Everybody said what a shame it was he married a dope like poor Doris—a girl that used to be a salesgirl in Marshall Field's in Chicago, that never finished high school, that couldn't read a serious book if her life depended on it, and every time she opened her mouth she used the wrong word or she mispronounced the right one.

"And the worst thing about her, everybody said, she couldn't get anywhere on time. For theater dates, for dinner at people's houses, Saul and Doris were always showing up late. And she was always apologizing because she forgot what time they were expected, or because she realized at the last minute that she was wearing the wrong dress, so she had to run back and change it. Poor Saul, everybody said—what an embarrassment for him to have such a dumb wife! And then—"

"Mother," Shirley broke in, "does this *really* have anything to do with that mink—"

"And then," Mom said, not even giving Shirley a glance, "your Aunt Doris died. All of a sudden she got sick, and a month later she

127

was dead. Only fifty-one years old—such a tragedy! Saul was so upset, for a long time he wouldn't go out of the house. But finally he started accepting invitations again—dinner parties, theater dates, and so on. And what a surprise everybody got! Everywhere he went, Saul got there late. Dinners got just as cold waiting for him as if Doris was still alive. So pretty soon the truth dawned on people. It was *Saul* who was inconsiderate and never showed up on time for his appointments. All these years it hadn't been Doris' fault at all. She used to pretend she was the guilty one, she used to let people blame this bad habit on her stupidity—because she loved her husband, she wanted to protect him and keep people from thinking bad things about him."

"But Mom, I don't see the point—"

"The point is, even a stupid person can love somebody and think up schemes to help him. Even a silly vain woman can care more about her husband than she cares about a mink coat. Smart people don't have a monopoly on making sacrifices. Waiter, I'll have some more coffee, please—and this time you'll make it hot?"

The coffee came, Mom sipped it and said it was hot enough, then she went on, "So now it's obvious, isn't it? Mrs. McCloskey, the doctor's wife, had trouble remembering people's names—even people she knew for years. Naturally she'd have trouble remembering the name of the woman that used to own her mink coat. Mrs. Janet Tannenbaum was the woman's name—but in Mrs. McCloskey's mind it could just as easy turn itself into Mrs. Juliet Tannenbaum."

"That seance!" I said. "When the ghost spoke through Mrs. Vivian's mouth—"

"The ghost's first words," Mom said, "if I'm remembering correctly, were 'This is Juliet Tannenbaum talking.' All right, even if you believe in ghosts you might have trouble believing in one that forgets her own first name! Somebody told Mrs. Vivian to speak in the ghost's voice, somebody wrote out those words for her to say—and paid her a nice bonus for putting on her act, enough so she could suddenly afford a new sofa at Macy's. And the somebody who did it was so vague and forgetful that she gave that ghost the wrong first name!"

MOM AND THE HAUNTED MINK

"But Mother," Shirley said, "that doesn't necessarily mean it was Mrs. McCloskey—"

"All right, if you want it, there's another piece of evidence that Mrs. McCloskey didn't really believe in the ghost. What did she do as soon as Mrs. Vivian's seance was over? She went to her husband's office, told him to sell the coat, then went off to her afternoon concert —where she wore the coat in public for the last time. So I'm asking you—if she really believed this coat had a ghost in it, if she really believed that threat which Mrs. Tannenbaum made, why didn't she take off the coat as soon as she could? Why wasn't she scared of wearing it another minute? How could she bring it to the concert and show it off to her friends without a worry in the world? Only one answer—this was a woman who knew that there wasn't any ghost."

"But if she staged that seance," I said, "she must've staged all those other things the ghost did. And I'll be— I mean, I don't see how she could have managed it!"

"It was simple. What *did* the ghost do, when you come right down to it? Most of the incidents—like the ghost pushing against her on the street, thumping at the closet door, failing off chairs in res-taurants—happened without any witnesses. And when the coat jumped off her back onto Mrs. Martineau's lawn—isn't it obvious that she *threw* it off her back? She didn't do it subconsciously, like Shirley said, she did it on purpose. She waited till nobody could see her do it except old Mrs. Harmon—who's very farsighted. Meaning that Mrs. Harmon could see the coat very clear while it was sailing through the air far away from her eyes, but she couldn't see anything except a blur while the coat was on Mrs. McCloskey's shoulders, *close* to her eyes. She couldn't see Mrs. McCloskey pulling off the coat and throwing it, but she *could* see it landing on the grass—so naturally she thought it got there by itself."

"And the night Mrs. McCloskey woke up her husband," I said, "and told him the coat had escaped from the closet and slid out to the front door—you mean she took it from the closet and wrapped it around that doorknob *before* she woke him up!"

"You still haven't explained the very first incident," Shirley said, "when the maid couldn't get the coat off its hanger—"

"That was probably a genuine accident," Mom said. "So a sleeve of the coat got caught on the hanger, just like Dr. McCloskey thought. And Mrs. McCloskey made a remark about Mrs. Tannenbaum's ghost. But later on, when she remembered this incident, it gave her the idea for everything else. It was her inspiration for the rest of the scheme."

"But *why*, Mom? What was her motive?"

"It's your Aunt Doris all over again, Davie. If a woman loves a man, she'll do anything she can to help him—even if it makes her look stupid. For years Mrs. McCloskey wanted a mink coat, and finally her husband bought her one, and she was happy with it at first. But pretty soon she began to notice certain things—he was selling rare books that he loved, cutting down on cigars, he was staying away from the steam bath. And maybe, out of curiosity, she accidentally looked through his papers and found out about his loan from the bank.

"And suddenly it came to her. 'These are the sacrifices he made to get me that mink coat!' Right away she hates the sight of that coat. She don't stop thinking it's beautiful—because she's a woman who's only human. But she's ashamed of herself for thinking so—because she's a woman who puts her husband first. All she wants to do now is get rid of the coat and give him back his money."

"But why such an absurd involved way of doing it?" Shirley said.

"How else could she do it? Could she tell him her real reason for getting rid of the coat? Maybe she's a stupid woman, but she knows what a blow this would be to his pride. Like a failure he'd feel, a no-good who couldn't afford to give his wife the things she wanted. So to save his pride she has to convince him she *don't* want that coat any more.

"If she says to him, 'I don't like the looks of it now!' he wouldn't believe her. But if she tells him she's got one of her crazy superstitions about it, if she invents a lot of incidents to account for this superstition, he *will* believe her. There isn't any silly notion he wouldn't think she was capable of—and she knows it."

" 'All right,' she decides, 'I'll make him believe I'm too scared to keep the coat. He'll think I'm acting like an idiot—but after all, he thinks that already. The important thing is, he'll get his books and his money back, and his pride will be saved!' "

Mom stopped, and gave a little sigh. "So that's what was haunting the coat—her love for her husband and her shame over spending his money."

"But Mom, the woman *was* murdered! The coat *has* disappeared!"

"Who's the murderer, is that what you're asking? Believe me, that's the easy part. That I knew right from the start. If you ever had to shop for a family, you'd know it also."

"Shop for a family!"

"You men at the Homicide Squad," Mom said, "you should all be forced to do your family shopping for a few weeks. It's because men don't have experience with such things that they're always such big suckers. Anything the salesgirl tells them they'll believe."

"What salesgirl? I don't see—"

"It's an old rule for shoppers, but it's still a good one—watch your step with a bargain. In this world nobody gives you something for nothing. If a two-dollar bag of oranges is selling for one dollar, you can automatically assume there are some rotten oranges in the bag. And if a fifteen thousand dollar mink coat is selling for five thousand dollars—"

"You think that coat was a fake, Mom? But the auction house valued Mrs. Tannenbaum's mink at—"

"Who says *that* Mrs. Tannenbaum's mink was the one Dr. McCloskey got? Who says Madame Rosa or Mr. Schultz or whatever his name is didn't slip a different mink out from his sleeve or maybe I should say a rabbit? This is a crime, if I'm not mistaken—he could go to jail for it, no?"

"He sure could!"

"So it isn't hard to imagine Mister Rosa's feelings when the doctor called him up and told him he was going to have the coat auctioned off. Nothing gets auctioned at those prices unless it's appraised first. Mr. Rosa *had* to get that coat back before any appraiser could look at it. So he sent the doctor out to Brooklyn on a wild goose chase, thinking that Mrs. McCloskey would be easier to convince alone. He showed up at the house and rang the bell. She let him in, and he tried to talk her into selling the coat back to him then and there. She wouldn't do it—he was a little too eager maybe—so they got into an argument and he lost his head and he smothered her with the first thing that came to his hand. It happened to be the mink coat."

"If we could prove that, Mom—"

"There was a box on the floor near her body, didn't you say so? A long box with a Madame Rosa label on it. You assumed this was the box that the coat originally came in, that Mrs. McCloskey was about to put the coat back in it for the auction house. But why should she hold onto that box for two months? She intended to keep the coat at the beginning, so naturally she threw its box away.

"The box you found near her body, Davie, was brought there by Mr. Rosa on the night of the murder, because he expected to carry the coat away in it. But after he killed Mrs. McCloskey he maybe panicked and ran away and forgot all about his box. Look it over— maybe it's got his fingerprints on it. Maybe somebody in his shop saw him leaving with it. I'm positive it'll be your proof."

I got to my feet. "I'll have Schultz picked up right now. Then we can start turning his place inside out."

So I left the table and phoned Homicide from the booth in the restaurant lobby. When I got back to the table I was just in time to hear Mom sighing. "It's like I mentioned earlier—mink is overrated. I've been wearing it for years, and believe me—"

And once again Shirley couldn't keep her mouth shut. "When did you ever wear mink, Mother? Just tell me one occasion."

Mom met Shirley's gaze, and her voice couldn't have been softer. "All my life I've been wearing it. I shut my eyes and run my hands over my shoulders and what do I feel? Mink—thick and soft, all the way down to my knees—the highest quality—"

"Oh, I see!" Shirley cried. "This mink is in your *imagination!*"

Mom spread her hands. "And why not? Isn't that the most beautiful kind?" For a moment there was a sad look on her face. But then the waiter came with the check. Mom took one look at it , and let out a yelp. "From now on, stove or no stove, we're eating up in the Bronx!"

MOM REMEMBERS

"ONE THING I'VE ALWAYS WANTED TO ASK you," said Inspector Millner to my mother. "How did you ever get interested in crime detection in the first place?"

Mom laughed and said, "From Mama, naturally. She taught me all I know."

This was a surprise to me. Mom never talked much about her parents or her childhood days. Nothing on earth is more boring, she used to say, than "an old lady looking backwards." So I put down my knife and fork and said, "Your mother had a talent for solving crimes, Mom?"

"A talent, he says! Did Einstein have a talent for adding up numbers? Does Van Kleinberg have a talent for playing the piano? All right, Mama never went to a college maybe, but as a detective she was a regular PH and D! If you're interested, I'll tell you about the first murder I ever ran up against. It was Mama who solved it—I only stood by and watched and learned—"

But before I go ahead, I'd better explain what led up to these reminiscences from Mom.

It was the fourth of May, a Wednesday night. Ordinarily Shirley and I go up to the Bronx to have dinner with Mom on Friday nights —but the fourth of May is a special date in Mom's life. It's the anniversary of her wedding to Papa. Shirley and I don't like her to be alone for that.

Forty-five years ago Mom and Papa were married. She was eighteen, and he was just twenty-one. Since childhood they had gone to school together and lived in the same tenement building on the lower

East Side; their families had come originally from the same little village in the old country. For a long time their parents had agreed —because that was how things were done in the old country—that the children would get married someday. It was no part of the arrangement that they had to be in love with each other—but strangely enough, they were in love with each other.

For over thirty years they lived together happily. They left the lower East Side and moved to the Bronx. They brought me, their only child, into the world. They saved enough money to send me to medical school. (I dashed their hopes by deciding, after I got out of college, to become a policeman.) Shortly afterward, while he was in his early fifties, my father died suddenly, his heart weakened by too many bills and too much nightwork and an inexhaustible capacity for worrying about other people's troubles. I'll never forget the look in Mom's eyes—though she struggled hard to keep me from noticing it. Even today, on the anniversary of their wedding, the shadow of that old pain flickers across her face.

Last May fourth Shirley and I brought Inspector Millner up to the Bronx with us. Inspector Millner is my boss at the Homicide Squad. He's a tall man with a bald head and bulldog features. His scowl can strike terror into the hearts of murderers, but sitting across the table from an unattached middle-aged lady with a coy look on her face, he becomes as shy and tongue-tied as an adolescent boy.

Anyway, Shirley and I have been trying for a few years now to get something going between Mom and him, and though there haven't been any serious developments yet, Mom always seems glad to see him. We thought it might cheer her up to see him on May fourth.

Sure enough she gave him a big hug in the foyer. "It's a pleasure to welcome you! Tonight is pot-roast, your favorite! If you don't make a glutton of yourself, I'll be insulted!"

A good beginning, I thought. Maybe Mom could get through the whole evening without any flickers of that old pain.

A little later, while we were eating her soup at the dining-room table, she said, "You like my matzoh balls, Inspector? It was the same with my Mendel. He used to tell me he could eat a hundred of them, and even the heartburn was worth it." Her voice began to shake a little. "Such a big appetite he had, for such a little sensitive-looking man—"

This was dangerous ground. Shirley and I spoke up at exactly the same moment.

"I saw a lovely coat at Macy's, Mother," Shirley said. "It was *you* all over."

"A new murder case broke this week, Mom," I said. "Inspector, why don't you tell her about it?"

"Coats can wait, darling," Mom said to Shirley, and then turned to Inspector Millner. "I'd be happy to hear about your new murder case, if you wouldn't mind taking the trouble."

The familiar glint of eagerness was in her eye. For a while, anyway, she would forget to be sad.

"I don't know why David bothered to mention it," the Inspector said. "It's a perfectly routine case. Nothing in it that could interest *you.*"

"Mom's interested in *all* our cases," I put in quickly.

"Well then—" Inspector Millner scratched his ear, a nervous habit whenever he had to make a speech in public "—this eighteen-year-old kid, his name is Rafael Ortiz, mugged and knifed a cab driver last night. It's the usual story. The kid's been hanging around with a bad crowd lately, staying out late at night, fighting with his parents. Sure enough he's finally got himself into serious trouble. Same damn things happening every day, all over the city—getting worse every year—"

"You're positive this boy is the guilty party?"

"Open-and-shut case. The man he knifed came to in the hospital and identified the kid just before he died. And there was an eye-witness too—a completely reliable witness. So you see, any ordinary cop could crack this case. It's a waste of your talents."

Mom blushed. I don't know anybody besides Inspector Millner who can make her blush. Shirley says it's a very hopeful sign.

So the conversation moved on to other things, and a little later—right after Mom served the pot-roast—Inspector Millner asked his question about how Mom ever got interested in crime detection. And she gave her answer—and we were back on dangerous ground again.

"I'll tell you about the first murder I ever ran up against," she said. "As I said, it was Mama who solved it. It was your Papa, Davie, who got Mama and me mixed up in it. My poor Mendel—"

That shake was in Mom's voice again. But I couldn't figure out how to break in and change the subject.

"When I tell you that Mama was a regular genius at solving crimes," Mom went on, "I don't mean she ever solved an actual murder—until the one that happened the day before our wedding. On the lower East Side in those days people didn't murder other people so much. In her imagination maybe, Mrs. Horowitz would *wish* that Mrs. Shapiro should drop dead, because Mrs. Shapiro is always bragging about her rich relatives uptown and acting like she's better than other people. But the minute after Mrs. Horowitz has such a terrible thought, she feels ashamed of herself, she begs God's pardon in *schul* and she makes some chicken soup for the Shapiro girl who's got the grippe.

"The point I'm making is, Mama didn't have any sons in the Homicide Squad or any sons at all—and they would've become lawyers or gone in for some other *normal* type of work. So the only crimes Mama got a chance to solve were the kind that don't get reported to the police or get written up in the newspapers.

"I'll give you a for instance. Mrs. Kinski from the third floor sells her husband's old Hebrew books while he's uptown working in the hat factory. She puts the money in a sugar can in her kitchen, and the next day it's gone. Nobody's been in that kitchen except the janitor's son to fix the water faucet—which is hopeless, because it's such an old faucet, what's left of it to fix? So everybody in the building is talking how the janitor has a son who's a thief.

"Then Mama steps in and asks a few questions and digs up a few pieces information and remembers something that happened when she a was a girl in the *shtetl* in Russia—and out comes the truth. Poor Mr. Kinski stole the money himself, so he could buy back his Hebrew books, which he loved more than anything on earth, including his wife.

"And another time—the little Glogauer girl, age nine, faints in school, and the doctor says it's from hunger, even though her mother, gives her a dime every day to buy a sandwich and an apple and a milk. The girl won't tell anybody what she's been doing with the money, and she cries if her mother asks her any questions.

"So Mama does a little poking here and a little poking there, and before the end of the week she uncovers a regular organized Chicago-gangster protection racket which is collecting dimes from all the little kids in the school—and who's running it? A half dozen eleven-year-old Al Caponies!

"This is the kind of crime that Mama was solving since I was a little baby, since as long as I could remember. The mind she had on her! If her opportunities had been better—if she could've been born in the lap from luxury and had a college education—if only she wasn't a widow with four daughters to bring up and living in a slum tenement and nothing but *tsouris* from the landlord! That wonderful mind, wasted on Delancey Street, to think of it sometimes it makes me almost cry!"

Mom trembled a little. Then she gave a shrug. "On the other hand, if life wasn't hard for Mama, maybe she never would have developed her wonderful mind in the first place. She *had* to be smart, and think faster and see more than other people—because how *else*, with no rich relatives, do you keep four daughters from starving and turning into old maids? When it's a matter of life and death to read the butcher's mind, believe me you learn how to be a mindreader!

"So anyway, all the time I was growing up from a little girl I am watching Mama and listening to her when she put that mind of hers to work. And also, you should know, I wasn't such a dope myself—so pretty soon, from picking up a few of her tricks, I got the idea I could do what *she* could do, I could be just as smart as *she* was.

"All right, I wouldn't try to hide from you—I got a swell head. And what excuse did I have? Only the excuse that I was eighteen years old. It's a bad disease, but thank God everybody grows out of it—except my sister Jennie who stayed eighteen till the day she died at sixty-three.

"Excuse me, I'll get back to that murder case forty-five years ago, when I finally got the swell head knocked out of me and found once for all that I couldn't be another Mama if I worked at it till I was a hundred."

Mom stopped, a little out of breath. When she went on talking, her voice was much softer. "Forty-five years ago—the day before my wedding. When I think what a close call it was—if it wasn't for Mama and her brains, would my wedding ever have happened? Would I be sitting here in the Bronx today? Davie, would *you* be sitting here, today? And the thirty-two years I had with my Mendel —those thirty-two happy years—"

A mist was coming over Mom's eyes—exactly what I had been afraid of. On May fourth you don't encourage Mom to reminisce. On May fourth you keep her as far away as possible from her memories.

So I broke in loudly. "Old murders don't interest me, Mom. It's *new* murders I care about. That's what the city pays me for after all. This Ortiz kid, the one who knifed the cab driver—I'm not sure it *is* an open-and-shut case, so I'd like to hear your opinion. Why don't you fill Mom in on the details, Inspector!"

"But the story about her wedding day—"

"You'll save it till later, won't you, Mom? We need your expert advice right now—we have to take advantage of this opportunity. Otherwise we wouldn't be doing our duty to the taxpayer."

I knew this strategy would work. The Taxpayer is a concept that always has a powerful effect on Inspector Millner's conscience.

He fidgeted a little and said, "Well—since David seems to think it's important—" He turned to Mom. "I'll tell you more about the Ortiz case. If it wouldn't bore you, that is."

Mom swallowed a piece of pot-roast and leaned forward politely. "When did it ever bore me?" she said.

"This Ortiz kid lives on the West in the Eighties," Inspector Millner began. "His parents came from Puerto Rico ten years ago, when Rafael was seven and his sister Inez was eight. Since then there have been two more kids, two little boys. The whole family lives in a run-down old firetrap off Amsterdam Avenue. Except the older sister,

Inez Ortiz—she moved into a hotel room downtown a year ago, because she and her father used to fight all the time."

"He's an easy man to fight with, Mr. Ortiz?" Mom said.

"He's an insignificant-looking little man. In his forties, but you'd think he was ten years older. He talks in a soft mumbling sort of voice, but all the neighbors say he's got a violent temper, particularly on Saturday nights when he does his drinking. He works in a shipping room down in the garment district, and the mother goes out five days a week as a cleaning woman, leaving her kids with the janitor's wife. In other words, it's no wonder that a kid growing up in a home like that gets himself into trouble."

"Plenty of them manage to stay out of trouble," Shirley said. "The emphasis in psychology today is far less on environmental factors and far more on old-fashioned will-power and individual effort—"

I could see Mom's nose twitching with annoyance. But she never let herself fight with Shirley when she had a guest at her table. So she smiled at Inspector Millner, and said, "You mentioned, I think, that it's only recently the boy started getting in trouble?"

"It began six months ago, when he got out of high school. Up till then he was a pretty decent kid, got good marks, held a job in the afternoons as a grocery delivery boy. His parents tell us he was never in a jam, and his teachers and the neighbors confirm that. Also there's no record on him down at Juvenile Court. He lives in a pretty tough neighborhood—there's a gang on the next block that we've been watching—but as far as we can tell, Rafael never had anything to do with them."

"So what changed him?"

"What changes every one of them? They lose hope, that's what. Sooner or later they get the message—high school, hard work, staying inside the law, where's it going to get them? The odds are a thousand to one they'll end up in a shipping room in the garment center, or washing dishes in a restaurant, or sorting mail for some city departments. They get the message, and it caves them in.

"Some of them turn into robots, like Rafael's father—nice quiet obedient machines all day long, then they take it out on their wives and kids at night. Some of them turn into vegetables—they float along on welfare, never hold a job more than a few months, drink too much, and blot out all thoughts of tomorrow. And some of them— the tough ones—try to hit back. Only how much damage can one Puerto Rican boy do to a System? Generally he lands himself in jail —or in the morgue.

"That's the direction Rafael's been taking since last winter. First he complained his job at the grocery store wasn't good enough for him—he had a right to be more than a delivery boy. So he quit and tried looking for something better—and it took him a month to realize he was hitting his head against a stone wall. He couldn't go back to the grocery store, though, or to anything like it—so he started hanging around the apartment.

"His father kept yelling at him and called him a bum—he yelled back and called his father a failure—his mother cried. So he stopped hanging around the apartment. Pretty soon he was showing up only for meals and staying out every night till after midnight, and when his father asked him where he'd been, he told the old man it was none of his business."

"He was spending his nights," Mom said, "with that gang you mentioned?"

"That's what his father thought. But the gang swears they had nothing to do with Rafael, and we can't find anybody who ever saw him with them. Whoever he's been hanging around with, it's some-body out of the neighborhood. Which makes it even worse."

"Could it be a girl maybe? Boys eighteen occasionally take an interest in the opposite sex."

"He has a girl all right. Her name is Rosa Melendez, and she lives half a block away from the Ortizes. Rafael is with her every Saturday and Sunday night, but on weekday nights she never sees him. She's asked him plenty of times where he goes, but all he ever tells her is that he's working on some kind of a 'big deal' and as soon as he pulls it off they'll have enough money to get married. Whenever she pushes him for more details, he gets mad at her and tells her that no man wants to marry a nagging woman."

140

"It sounds to me as if he's got another girl somewhere," Shirley said, "and he doesn't want Rosa to know about her."

"It's possible," the Inspector said. "But for what it's worth, Rosa doesn't think so. She's been worried sick about him, she admits she's suspected all sorts of awful things—but not once, she says, has she thought he was two-timing her. And I believe her. Besides, the 'mystery girl' theory doesn't fit with a certain crazy story the boy's father told us."

"What story?" Mom said.

"About a week ago the boy's mother got sick—a bad case of this virus that's going around—and she had to stay in bed for a couple of days. Well, in the middle of the afternoon her TV set went on the blink—"

"These people are poverty-stricken," Shirley said, "but they can still afford to have a television set?"

"If you're poverty-stricken," Mom said, "you can't afford *not* to have television. How else can you forget for a while that you're poverty-stricken?"

"Anyway, Rafael fooled around the back of the set with a screwdriver," the Inspector said, "and managed to get it working again. That night he went out after dinner the same as usual—after the usual fight with his father because he wouldn't say where he was going—and around ten o'clock he called up from outside to find out if the TV was still working.

"He talked to his father, who asked him where he was calling from. This started another argument—but while it was going on, Ortiz heard voices in the background, from his son's end of the line. They were very low at first, and Ortiz couldn't make out what they were saying. Then one of the voices, a man's voice, got louder, and kind of angry. Ortiz heard very clearly what he said. 'Who's scared of the dicks? If any copper gets in my way, I'll mow him down!' A moment later Rafael hung up the phone."

"And his father told you all this?" Shirley said. "Voluntarily—knowing how incriminating it was?"

"I'm afraid he did. Old Ortiz is very bitter about the boy. 'He killed a man, let him take his punishment.' The mother, of course, is

141

just the opposite. She won't hear a word said against the boy. 'My Rafael wouldn't hurt anybody,' she keeps saying. And for her sake —I admit it—I wish our case wasn't so strong. . . ."

The Inspector's voice trailed off mournfully. After a moment Mom said, "What about Mrs. Ortiz's television set? Was it working all right when the boy called up?"

"Good heavens, Mother," Shirley said, "what on earth does that matter?"

"Still I'd like to know."

"The TV was working fine," Inspector Millner said. "The boy's always had a knack for mechanical things. It's a shame he'll never be able to do anything with it now."

"Now?" Mom said.

The Inspector's face tightened. "Two nights ago he threw away his whole life. Around eleven a cab driver named Dominic Palazzo —a little fellow in his sixties, five times a grandfather—let off a fare at Broadway and Eighty-sixth Street, then started east. At Amsterdam Avenue he was hailed by a kid—short, thin, dark hair which was almost as long as a girl's—that was Palazzo's description. Sounds like most of these crazy kids nowadays, I admit it. The kid got in the cab and told Palazzo to take him downtown—and spoke with a Spanish accent.

"Well, after a couple of blocks, when they came to a dark empty stretch, the kid pulled a knife, held it against Palazzo's neck, and ordered him to stop the cab and hand over his cash. It seems Palazzo had been hit by robbers twice in the last year and he couldn't afford to take another loss. So he slammed down on the brakes, hoping to knock the kid off balance and grab his knife away from him. But before Palazzo could even turn his head, the kid stabbed that knife into the back of his neck. Then he jumped out of the cab, ran down the street, and disappeared around the corner. Palazzo was bleeding badly, but didn't die till two hours later, in the hospital. He had time to make a positive identification."

"You brought the Ortiz boy to the hospital?" Mom said.

"Not the boy himself. We went to his home to pick him up—but he'd left after dinner as usual, and he wasn't back yet. We got a photograph of him from his mother—his high school graduation picture and Palazzo took one look it and said, 'That's him!' ''

"Something is puzzling me a little," Mom said. "How come you went to the boy's home to pick him up such a short time after the stabbing? What made you suspect him?"

"There was an eyewitness. He came out of an all-night hamburger joint on the far corner just after Palazzo started yelling. He saw the boy running down the street and recognized him."

"In the dark, from a block away, with the boy's back turned?"

"It's true this witness didn't actually see the boy's face. But he recognized the general build and coloring—and especially what the boy was wearing. A few months ago, the boy bought a leather jacket —bright red, with a black dragon's head on the back—and a black leather motorcycle cap, and he's been wearing this crazy outfit as often as possible ever since. His father told him he looked like a hoodlum in it—so naturally that encouraged him to keep on wearing it.

"Anyway, his parents and some others say that he had this jacket and this cap on when he left his home after dinner on the night of the murder—and our witness clearly saw this same jacket and cap on the boy running away from Palazzo's cab. That, plus Palazzo's identification of the photograph, clinched the case as far as we were concerned. We waited in front of the boy's building till twelve thirty, when he came walking down the street, whistling to himself as if he didn't have a care in the world. Sure enough, he was wearing the red jacket and the black cap. So we pulled him in."

"And he confessed to the crime?" Mom said.

"He *still* hasn't confessed. He swears he wasn't anywhere near Amsterdam Avenue and the Eighties all night long. We asked him where he *had* been, and he said he'd been to the movies with his sister Inez. He picked her up downtown—she works as a waitress in a Times Square restaurant, and her hotel is a couple of blocks away— and they went to see a Western double bill together.

"We contacted her, and asked her if she'd been to the movies with him that night. She said she had. Then we got a little tricky—we asked her to describe the two science-fiction pictures they had seen.

She started talking about monsters and spaceships—well, the upshot was, they both admitted the alibi was a phony. But Rafael still won't admit he killed the cab driver—and he still won't tell us where he spent the night, or where he's been spending most of his nights in the last few months. Well, under the circumstances, what are we supposed to think?"

The Inspector spread his hands helplessly. There was no missing the look of misery on his face.

Then, in a gentle voice, Mom said, "But this evidence against the boy—is it really so open-and-shut? The cab driver picked up a boy on a dark street, and two minutes later this boy stabbed him from behind—so how positive could the poor man's identification be?"

"Palazzo had a good eye and a good memory, Mom," I said. "A year ago, when he was robbed the first time, he didn't get any better look at the thief—but he picked him out two weeks later from the line-up."

"Besides," the Inspector said, "our other witness saw the red jacket and the black cap."

"Couldn't more than one boy in New York have a red jacket with a dragon on it? Maybe this Ortiz belongs to a gang, and this jacket and cap are their uniform."

"No gang in Rafael's neighborhood wears such a uniform," the Inspector said. "Or anywhere else in the city, as far as we can discover. If there *was* such a gang we'd be bound to know about it. That's why these kids wear these crazy outfits in the first place—so they can show them off in public."

Mom frowned. Then she said, "And this witness who claims he saw the boy's jacket running away from the crime? Can you trust him, this witness? Maybe he killed the cab driver himself, and he's trying to put the blame on an innocent party. Maybe it's a framing-up."

"Our witness is above suspicion," Inspector Millner said.

"Excuse me—" Mom gave a little smile, with just a touch of condescension in it "—when you've seen some of the things I've seen in my life, you stop believing that any flesh-and-blood human being is above suspicion. The richest member of our synagogue before the

144

War—a man who gave thousands of dollars to charity, a man with white hair and double-breasted suits—but when five hundred dollars were missing from the Building Fund—"

"Mom," I broke in, "even *you* will have to believe this witness." I took a breath and went on, "The fact is, *I'm* the witness."

Not many times in my life have I seen Mom look surprised. This was one of those times. "Davie—you're making a joke?"

"I wish I were. Last week a man in the Ortizes' building beat his wife to death. He confessed right afterwards, but I had to get statements from the other tenants. When I talked to the Ortiz couple, Rafael was in the room all the time. Heckling me, making cracks about cops—nothing I'm not used to, you understand, but the incident helped me to remember the boy. And to remember the jacket he was wearing.

"Two nights ago, around eleven, I finished my questioning and went across the street for a hamburger and a cup of coffee. I heard yells from the street and went out to see what was up—and I saw the boy running away from the cab. I didn't go after him because it looked as if the cab driver needed help right away. Besides, I knew I could always pick up the kid later on. Take my word for it, Mom— I would've recognized that red jacket anywhere."

Mom frowned harder. Finally she said, "So I believe you, Davie. Naturally. What else? Only—something about this case keeps itching at me—"

A gleam of hope lighted up Inspector Millner's face. "The boy didn't do it? If I could tell that to his mother—if you had some proof—"

"Proof I don't have. Only an idea. Not even an idea—a comparison."

"A comparison with what?"

"With what—?" Suddenly that shadow, that flicker of pain, was on Mom's face. "This murder—it's like the first murder case I ever ran up against. This Ortiz boy—like Mendel he is. Like my poor Mendel, forty-five years ago—"

My God, we were on dangerous ground again! I didn't know exactly how we had got there, but I certainly intended to get us off.

MY MOTHER, THE DETECTIVE

"Forget about that old murder, Mom," I said. "Please keep your mind on *this* murder, will you?"

"What else am I doing—?" Mom said. "Don't you follow me, Davie? This murder right now, that murder forty-five years ago—they could almost be the *same* murder. I couldn't solve the new one if I wouldn't think about the old one—"

I saw that I was beaten and had no choice but to give up gracefully. "All right, Mom, if that's how you want it," I said. "Tell us about that old murder."

Mom folded her hands in her lap and smiled around at us all. "Since you're asking me, I'll tell you," she said. "Only don't let the pot-roast get cold, please. Eat, Inspector—eat, Shirley darling—you, Davie, I don't have to encourage, you'll eat no matter what. And while you're all eating, I'll talk."

"First I have to tell you about my Mendel," Mom said. "Your Papa, Davie, was a wonderful man. But maybe most people nowadays wouldn't agree with me. The things in him which were wonderful aren't so fashionable no more—and come to think of it, who knows when they ever were? A big business brain he wasn't—a big personality that told jokes and slapped people on the back he wasn't—a face like Rudolph Valentino and a body like Tarzan he didn't have. You only had to give one look at him, and you knew the day would never come when he'd make a million dollars. So phooey with him! Who cares about such a *schlimazl*? But this *schlimazl* was kind-hearted and considerate, and he never got mad at people and never said insulting things, and the way he bounced you on his knee, Davie, when you were a little baby—the look of happiness on his face! Plenty millionaires, believe me, live for eighty years and never get such a happy look on their faces, not even when they're adding up their bank books. So for all these things I fell in love with this *schlimazl* which, in the opinion of a lot of people, including my sister Jennie with the empty head, made me a *schlimazl* too.

"At the age fifteen Mendel was brought by his father and mother to America from the old country. His father was a rabbi. Such a fine-looking man, with a long black beard and eyes that caught on fire

146

when he got angry at somebody and a deep voice that could fill a whole synagogue and also a couple of blocks outside! Into the same building he moved as Mama and my sisters and me—two floors above us—and pretty soon he was made the rabbi of our *schul*. And I have to admit it—everybody respected and admired Mendel's Papa, but also everybody was a little bit afraid of him. Because nobody was as strict as he was for keeping the old ways, obeying the old laws.

"For instance, maybe one of the women—strictly accidental, you understand—would get a milk dish mixed up with a meat dish, and she wouldn't find out about it till just before dinnertime. So instead of throwing everything out and starting the dinner all over again, maybe she would say a little apology to God and serve the food to her family and forget to mention her mistake. All right, was this such a big sin? Did she do it to save herself trouble?

"No, she did it to keep her loved ones from going hungry. So wouldn't God forgive one little accident when it's a question of a hard-working husband and growing children who need their nourishment? Yes, God would forgive but not Mendel's Papa! At *schul* on Friday night this poor woman would stay as far away from him as she could. If he once looked her straight in the face with those black fiery eyes, she was positive he could see right through to the terrible secret in her heart.

"Mendel, when he got off the boat in New York City, didn't know one word from English. Yiddish and Hebrew were all he knew. His first year in this country, till he learned the language, wasn't easy for him. And I wouldn't lie to you, his English never *was* exactly from Harvard College. He could say what was on his mind, and understand what others said, but all his life, till the day he died, he spoke with an accent—and his last day on this earth, in the hospital bed, he forgot all the English he had learned, and all his words were Yiddish.

"Just the same, he went to school at P.S. 84 till he was seventeen, and then he went to work for Friedman and Son, Men's Underwear. He was a cutter in the shop. Not exactly the type work his father had in mind for him—his father wanted him to be a rabbi, a scholar, and follow in the family tradition.

147

"But first of all, Mendel wasn't the scholarly type—his pleasure was from people, not from books. And second of all, America isn't like the old country. Back in the *shtetl a* young man that spent all his days studying the Talmud was a hero. He gave pride to everybody, and if he needed food to eat and clothes on his back, who wouldn't be glad to contribute?

"But here in America, on Delancey Street, it was hard enough finding the food and clothes for your own children—and who needed scholars anyway? Did the American newspapers ever print stories about any scholars? Did you ever read where a scholar won a prize or made a speech or got elected to anything? To be a success in America you had to be a businessman or a professional man or a star in the movies. So who was going to make contributions for Mendel to spend his life with his nose in the Talmud?

"His own father couldn't do it because let's face it, a rabbi on the lower East Side in those days wasn't getting the type salary, with bonuses and a house and complimentary trips to Israel, that these famous important rabbis with vests and no hair on their faces are getting today. So Mendel went to work as a cutter in Friedman and Son's shop, and not even his Papa, no matter how angry he got, could do anything about it.

"Three years he worked in Friedman's shop. He was a good cutter, my Mendel, and also he had bigger ambitions. And all the time I was in love with him, and he was in love with me. So you're asking, what were we waiting for? For two things only—that I should be eighteen years old, and that Mendel should save enough money so he could quit his job, set up a tailor shop on his own. And since he didn't drink or smoke, or strut around in fancy clothes, or go out with no-good women, with Jezebels, that only show an interest in a man if he spends a lot of money on them—since his idea of a happy evening was to come down two floors and play three-handed pinochle with Mama and me—his savings in the bank were growing very nicely, even though Friedman and Son were, God knows, not exactly showering him with riches. Finally, when I had my eighteenth birthday, Mendel said that the time was come to look around for a store to rent—and he talked to my Mama, and I talked to his Papa, and the wedding day was set for the fourth of May. Which only goes to show—people can make their plans, but God might have a plan of his own up his sleeve."

Mom stopped for a moment and gave a little shudder. "God's plan was to play on Mendel and me a little joke. Not such a funny joke, in my opinion—but since when are we supposed to appreciate God's sense of humor? The joke went like this—the trouble that suddenly came to my Mendel, and nearly stopped him from having a wedding or anything else in his life, was brought on his head by one of those no-good women, those Jezebels that he never would have anything to do with.

"Jezebel, naturally, wasn't her name. Sadie Katz was her name. All right, it don't sound so glamorous. In the movies you never saw a vamp named Sadie Katz. In the history books you never read how any Sadie Katz was a king's girl friend and changed the fate of a nation. Well, it's like William Shakespeare said in one of those plays that they made into a movie. 'What's in a name? A girl could be called Rosie or any other name and still she wouldn't smell so sweet.' Hundreds of years ago he wrote those words, and he could've been talking about Sadie Katz!

"She worked by Friedman and Son the same as Mendel. She was on the sewing machines, so she wasn't even on the same floor with Mendel. But she liked to walk around the shop a lot, and give a look-over at everybody that happened to be wearing pants. Half the time her sewing machine was turned off, and she was wandering here and there, wiggling her hips and blinking her long eyelashes at anybody who enjoyed such spectacles. And plenty enjoyed, believe me—including Grossfeld the foreman—a man in his forties with five children and a sick wife! But how else, if it wasn't for Grossfeld, did Sadie Katz produce such a small amount of work and still not get fired?

"She was a dark-haired girl—except occasionally when she felt like being a blonde—and originally she was from Lithuania. A Litvak —so what could you expect? No, excuse me, I shouldn't have made such a stupid remark. The Litvaks are the same as anybody else—

prejudices I haven't got, believe me. It's only that something comes over me when I think of that Sadie Katz. Even after all these years—

"Anyway, she was working in the shop for six, seven months when finally she met my Mendel. And after that there practically wasn't a day she didn't throw herself at him. She went up behind him while he was cutting and she mussed his hair. She told him how good-looking he was. She left the shop when he did, and brushed against him in the doorway, and walked along the street with him. She dropped hints—they were as big as atom bombs, those hints—that any time he wanted to he could call her up and take her out.

"No, don't interrupt—I can see the question on your faces. Didn't I just get through saying that Mendel was no Rudolph Valentino, and no John D. Rockefeller either? So why should this Sadie Jezebel, this Delilah Katz, take such an interest in him? For such a girl, what was the attraction of a homely little man that got his fun from playing pinochle with his fiancée and his future mother-in-law?

"The answer is that Mendel had one attraction for Sadie Katz which none of the other men in the shop had—Mendel wouldn't pay any attention to her. To her charms and her beauty—though frankly I could never see that she was so beautiful—he was positively a blind man. When she mussed his hair, he squirmed—but from embarrassment, not from excitement. When she told him she wanted to go out with him, he thanked her—politely because Mendel could never hurt anybody's feelings—but explained he was engaged to get married, so he didn't go out with any girls except me.

"Well, the truth was, Sadie Katz never ran up against anything like this before. She was used to the men hanging out their tongues for her, throwing themselves under her feet, hopping up and down when she told them to hop. That some poor little cutter, some nobody without a penny to his name, should be able to do without her so nicely—this was a blow to her pride. She couldn't sleep peaceful again till she got Mendel to hang out his tongue for her like everybody else.

"Meanwhile, naturally, she didn't give up her social life from aggravation over Mendel. At the rooming house where she lived, the landlady said she went out practically every night of the week with some man or other. Sometimes he'd come and pick her up, and sometimes she'd get all dressed up and go out alone, without telling anybody who she was going to—and at two o'clock in the morning she'd come waltzing in, still alone but singing to herself. And that same morning she'd get to the shop an hour late or even more—only you can take three guesses if that *noodnick* Grossfeld ever bawled her out!

"Well, this is how it went until the night before my wedding. May third, forty-five years ago—when all of a sudden Sadie Katz ended up the way so many Jezebels and Delilahs end up. She got herself murdered."

Mom gave one of her dramatic pauses. Then she looked around the table, "What's the matter?" she asked. "Why isn't anybody eating? The pot-roast isn't up to the usual standard?"

We all assured Mom that the pot-roast was delicious, and we started eating again. She relaxed, and went on with her story.

"On May third, at six in the evening, there was a party in Mendel's honor. A bachelor party, with jokes and speeches and drinking toasts to say goodbye to Mendel being an unmarried man. Ten or twelve people were at this party—Mendel's closest friends from the shop, and also Grossfeld the foreman, who wasn't such a close friend actually but how do you tell the foreman you don't want him at your party? Everybody chipped in with a little money to buy Mendel a wedding present—a fountain pen with a gold clip and his initials on it. Right then and there Mendel took it out and wrote with it, and then he cried a little—from pleasure, you understand.

"This party was held on the first floor of the shop, which had Mr. Friedman's private office and the showroom for the out-of-town buyers. Mr. Friedman, from respect and liking for Mendel, let them use the showroom—and he himself made an appearance at the party near the end. He made a speech, calling Mendel a fine human being and a first-class cutter. Just between us, I think Friedman still had hopes he could keep Mendel from quitting his job and opening up a tailor shop—because even in those days, with sweatshops and no unions, a good cutter wasn't so easy to find.

151

"But excuse me, I don't want to do Friedman any injustice. He was a man with his heart in the right place. Being the Son in Friedman and Son—the old man died years before—he had an idea the employees didn't respect him like they used to respect his father. So to make up for this he wore those expensive suits, he lived uptown on Park Avenue, he played golf, he made long-winded speeches, and sometimes he was a little highhanded in his business methods.

"But deep down underneath, this wasn't the real Friedman. Didn't he give Mendel a whole two days off for his honeymoon? Didn't he tell his wife—she used to be Stella Plotkin from Stanton Street when she worked for him as his secretary, but now she was Stella Friedman with two mink coats—to tell their cook to bake a small-size chocolate cake for Mendel's party? Didn't he provide the champagne himself, at his own expense? Imported French champagne it wasn't—if I remember correctly, it was champagne from Newark, New Jersey—but still it was a nice gesture on Friedman's part.

"How many times afterwards did I wish that this champagne had been nothing but grape juice! If it wasn't for this champagne, Mendel never would have had this trouble. The fact is, he wasn't used to drinking alcohol. A little wine on the Sabbath, this was his limit. And if he took more than one glass, he was dizzy for the rest of the night.

"But at the party, with everybody drinking toasts and wishing him luck, how could he sit there and not drink back at them? So by the time the party was over—and it only lasted an hour—Mendel had five glasses champagne in him, and the world was doing flip-flops in front of his eyes, and he was talking a lot louder than usual. Without beating around the bushel, Mendel was drunk.

"He was so drunk that he couldn't walk home all by himself. So Grossfeld the foreman and a couple other fellows had to help him walk along the street. They did a lot of singing and shouting on the way, and Mendel did as much as anybody else. A block or two from home it suddenly came into his head that it wouldn't be such a good idea if his Papa smelled champagne on his breath. I told you already that Mendel's Papa thought the orthodox ways and traditions were more important than anything on earth. And one of the oldest traditions is that a Jewish boy shouldn't get drunk. He shouldn't be a Prohibitionist either, you understand—he can take a *schnapps* or two for relaxation—but he never goes overboard and loses his head and makes a fool of himself. If Mendel's Papa, a rabbi, found out that his own son was drunk, what a *megilla* there'd be!

"So Mendel stopped at a candy store and bought a roll of peppermints for a nickel—his idea was to chew the peppermints and take the champagne smell off his breath. But he was in such a condition that he couldn't stick to this idea. He put the peppermints in his pocket, along with the change from his dollar bill, and he forgot all about them.

"Anyhow, Mendel and his friends and Grossfeld reached our building, and Mendel walked up the stoop, and then he turns to say goodbye to his friends. He not only says goodbye, he makes a speech. His voice is so loud and his gestures are so funny that children come running to look at him and people stick their heads out of windows up and down the block. Mendel waves his arms and shouts at them, 'I'm a happy man! I'm in love, and I'm getting married! Look at the beautiful fountain pen my friends gave me! Also they gave me five glasses champagne!'

"And at this moment, like she was dropped there in a whirlwind, Sadie Katz is suddenly standing next to Mendel. From the shop she followed him, and now she can't resist the temptation—she puts her arms around him, gives him a big kiss on the mouth, and says to him so everybody can hear, 'You're a free man until tomorrow, Mendel. So why don't you drop in tonight and visit me?' And she runs off.

"Then Mendel goes upstairs to his apartment—and his Papa is waiting for him at the door. Right away, as soon as he got a look at his Papa's expression, Mendel was sober again. From the window Mendel's Papa had seen what was going on in the street, and now he was angrier than Mendel could ever remember him—and Mendel's Papa was a man who got angry two or three times every day. So for half an hour Mendel's Papa called him terrible names—a drunkard, a worse than that—and then, like a miracle out of the sky, Mendel did something he never did before in his life.

153

MY MOTHER, THE DETECTIVE

"He answered his Papa back. He argued, he contradicted. He said he wasn't a drunkard, he said his Papa was old-fashioned and narrow-minded, he said he had a right to live his own life. He didn't say these things maybe with the eloquence of a Jeremiah, a Franklin D. Roosevelt, a Rabbi Stephen Wise—but he said them, this is what counts. After twenty-one years where did he get the courage? Maybe it was the champagne. Or maybe, on the day before his wedding, a man stops being afraid of things, because he don't think anything worse could happen to him.

"So the argument got louder and angrier, and finally Mendel's Papa called him a sinner and a transgressor and ordered him into his room. And Mendel said, 'Why should I go into my room? It's early yet, the night hasn't even begun—I have to go out and do some more sinning and transgressing!' Then, while his Papa shook a fist at him and his poor Mama moaned and squeezed her hands, Mendel went marching out of the apartment.

"It was eight o'clock at night when he left. It was after midnight when he got back. His Mama heard him closing the front door, then going to the bathroom, then making noises like he was being sick in the sink. Then she heard him going to bed. A little later she sneaked into his room and saw him fast asleep, with his clothes thrown all over the furniture. So she emptied the pockets and hung up his suit, and sneaked out of his room again.

"The next morning the police came and arrested Mendel for strangling Sadie Katz to death, some time between nine thirty and eleven the night before."

Mom gave another one of her pauses. She has a genius for knowing when to make her listeners wait.

She ate a piece of pot-roast, washed it down with a mouthful of water, and went on. "Sadie Katz lived in Mrs. Spiegel's rooming house on Avenue A. It was a five story building, and if it ever saw better days, they must have been before the American Revolutionary War. Sadie Katz had a room on the second floor, which was just about big enough for a bed and a basin. Mrs. Spiegel lived on the first floor, with Mr. Spiegel, who went out every day and sold old clothes from his pushcart while Mrs. Spiegel took care of the rooming

154

house. They came from Germany five years before, the Spiegels, and looked down their noses at anybody who came from Russia or Poland. They pretended to be cultured and intellectual. Spiegel was always reading German books, and the two of them went three or four times a year to the theater.

"On May third, according to the Spiegels, Sadie Katz got back to the rooming house at seven o'clock—which must have been a few minutes after she made such a spectacle of herself in front of our building. She went up to her room, and they could smell a piece of meat cooking on her hot plate. In Mrs. Spiegel's rooming house there was only one telephone—it was on the wall in the ground-floor hallway, and the roomers had to put a nickel in if they wanted to make a call. Sometimes people from outside would call this phone—which happened at ten minutes after eight on the night of May third. Mrs. Spiegel answered the ring, and a voice—a low whispering kind of voice, like somebody with a cold—asked to speak with Sadie Katz. Mrs. Spiegel yelled upstairs for Sadie, and went back to her apartment where she was giving Spiegel a knockwurst dinner.

"She closed her apartment door, naturally, but not all the way—maybe by accident. The Spiegels could hear every word Sadie Katz was saying on the phone. 'What a surprise to hear from *you!*' she said. 'You want to see me tonight? I'm flattered,' she said. 'No, I won't meet you outside. I'm tired, and I want to spend a nice evening at home. So why don't you come over here?'

"There was a long pause, and then Sadie sounded a little angry. 'Why should anybody see you?' she said. 'You'll ring the front door-bell, I'll come down and let you in myself. And what if somebody *does* see you? Am I a social outcast or something? Is it a crime to pay me a visit?' Then she gave a laugh and said, 'What are you afraid of? You're still a free man, aren't you? You can do what you like!'

"And then she said, 'All right, I'll expect you in about an hour.' Then she hung up the phone, knocked on the Spiegels' door, and told them she was expecting a visitor tonight, and she'd appreciate it if they let her open the front door when the bell rang. Then she went upstairs to her room.

155

"It was nearly nine thirty when the front doorbell rang. Mrs. Spiegel opened her door and started out to the lobby—but Sadie Katz appeared on the stairs at the same time. 'I'll get it, thank you,' she said, and she deliberately waited till Mrs. Spiegel went back into her apartment. A few seconds later the Spiegels heard the front door opening, then they heard Sadie's voice, loud and cheerful, and another voice, very low and muffled—and then they heard two pairs of feet climbing the stairs. But they never even caught a glimpse at Sadie's visitor.

"A little later the Spiegels went to bed, because Spiegel had to get up at the cracking of dawn and go out with his pushcart, if he expected to compete with the other old clothes peddlers from the neighborhood. So they slept all night and woke up at five o'clock. At six o'clock Mrs. Spiegel saw Spiegel out the front, then she went upstairs to give a knock on Sadie's door—she did this every morning, so Sadie would wake up in time for work. Only this morning there was no answer to the knock.

"Mrs. Spiegel tried the door, and it wasn't locked. She went into the room and saw Sadie Katz lying on the floor. Sadie was wearing her fanciest clothes—what she'd been wearing at nine thirty the night before—but her make-up was smeared, her sleeve was torn, and her tongue was sticking out. So Mrs. Spiegel started screaming.

"May fourth this was. The morning of my wedding day. Only before this morning was over it looked like there wouldn't be any wedding.

"The police came to Sadie Katz's room and examined the body and heard from the Spiegels about the phone call and the visitor. Especially they were interested in one part of that phone conversation—'You're still a free man, aren't you? You can do what you like.'

"Who could Sadie have said these words to, except somebody who pretty soon would *stop* being a free man—in fact, somebody who was on the verge of getting married? So the police went to Delancey Street, got Mendel out of bed, and arrested him."

"The evidence seems pretty flimsy," I said. "We wouldn't arrest a man on evidence like that today."

"Excuse, me, I forgot to mention," Mom said. "There was one other piece evidence. On the floor of Sadie's room was a big mess—things that fell there from the struggle with the murderer. Part of this mess was a new fountain pen, with a gold clip, and with Mendel's initials on it."

Inspector Millner sucked in his breath. There was a look of concern on his face—as if he were Papa's closest friend, and the murder had happened only yesterday.

"But it was even worse than that," Mom went on. "The police asked Mendel where he was between eight o'clock, when he left his apartment, and after midnight, when he came home again. Mendel said he didn't know. He got on the subway and stayed on it till he felt like getting off—he didn't even notice what stop. Then he walked along the street for a while, only he couldn't say what street—some people passed by him and laughed at him for having his hat on. Then he sat on a bench in a little park—he couldn't say what park, he couldn't say how long. Finally he got up and went back to the subway—but it turned out he didn't have any money in his pockets—so he walked all the way home.

"Then the police showed him his fountain pen, and he admitted it was his and looked surprised that it wasn't still in his pocket. The police told him they weren't satisfied with his story—who would be?—but Mendel wouldn't change it.

"And then Mendel did something that made his case practically hopeless. 'I'm guilty,' he said. 'I broke the law, I deserve to be punished' And he went up to his Papa and got down on his knees. 'Forgive me, Papa, I'm a sinner and a transgressor, just like you called me!'

"Naturally the police pounced on this. 'Are you confessing the murder?' they said to him. 'You're admitting you went to the girl's room and tried to make love to her—and when she rejected you, you flew into a rage and killed her?'

"But Mendel just blinked at them and said, 'I didn't kill anybody,' and went on saying how guilty he was. He went on saying it all the way to jail."

MY MOTHER, THE DETECTIVE

Mom broke off with a sad little smile. "An hour later, while I was trying on my wedding dress, they broke the news to me. I started shouting that I had to get to the jail, and see my Mendel and comfort him in his time of trouble.

"Mama tried to calm me down. 'Don't be in such a hurry taking off your wedding dress,' she said. 'If you're not careful, you'll tear it.' But she didn't insist very hard on this. Because the same thought was in her head and mine—the chances were that this dress would never be needed."

Through the window we heard a woman yelling. "Herbie, get up here right this minute, or you're in bad trouble! You hear me, Herbie?"

It broke the spell. It pulled us out of the lower East Side of forty-five years ago, with its ramshackle tenements and narrow streets, back to the Grand Concourse and the TV antennas and the faint humming of air conditioners.

"For heaven's sake, Mother," Shirley said, "what *happened?*"

"What happened?" The sadness went out of Mom's smile. Some of the old tartness came back to her voice. "We're all here tonight, aren't we? So that's pretty good proof that the wedding dress was used."

"You cleared your husband of suspicion?" Inspector Millner said. "You solved the murder?"

"How could I be in any condition to solve anything? At eighteen years old, even under ordinary circumstances—even if the man you love *hasn't* been put in jail—you're slightly hysterical. So it wasn't me who did the solving, it was Mama.

"Right away, as soon as I was out of my wedding dress and back in my normal clothes, Mama made me sit quiet on the sofa and gave me a glass seltzer water and took hold of my hand.

" 'All right,' she said, 'let's take one minute to talk over this situation. You wouldn't do Mendel any good by running down to the jail and crying over him. All you'll do is get him wet. What's needed now is figuring out some way to prove he's innocent.'

MOM REMEMBERS

" 'Mama, you believe he's innocent?' I said, and if somebody gave me a million dollars I couldn't have been more grateful.

" 'Naturally I believe,' Mama said. 'A nice boy like Mendel that wouldn't even cheat in a pinochle game—if he drank all the champagne in New York he couldn't play around with another girl behind your back. And murder? With his kind heart and his weak stomach, he couldn't murder a cockroach in the sink.' Then Mama looked at me very hard. 'And you, baby? You don't believe he's innocent? You love him, and you've got doubts?'

"I swore to Mama that I had no doubts. This was the truth—but let's face it, it was still a relief to find out that Mama agreed with me. All by itself my opinion was strictly from the emotions of a girl in love. With Mama behind it this opinion suddenly had some sense in it—there was even a possibility we could make other people believe it too.

" 'So let's go over the facts,' Mama said, rubbing her hands together exactly like she did before she 'went over the facts' about Mrs. Kinski's sugar can. So for the next half hour Mama and I told each other three or four times what the police and the neighbors and Mendel's mother had told us. I concentrated hard on every bit of it, trying to see it with Mama's eyes and think about it with Mama's mind. How many times had I said to myself that I could solve problems just as good as Mama solved them! So here was my chance, with my Mendel's life at stake. Now was the time to prove I wasn't strictly a bag of talk.

"After half an hour I didn't have an idea in my head. But suddenly Mama gave a big smile and nodded her head a couple times. 'Good, good, I'm beginning to get a thought,' she said. '*Now* you can run down to the jail and cry over Mendel, baby. But also don't forget to ask him a certain question I've got in mind. And then you should drop in on Grossfeld, the foreman at the shop, and ask *him* a question. And another question you should ask the Spiegels at the rooming house. And in the meantime I'll go upstairs and give a little sympathy to Mendel's poor Mama and Papa and while I'm there, I'll ask *them* a question too.'

"Then Mama told me what her questions were—and none of them made any sense to me. But I agreed to ask them anyway—

because in those days when a mother told a child to do something, you did it, and you didn't put up any argument.

"Down at the jail they let me talk to Mendel in a long room with a table between us. First I told him I loved him and believed in him. Then I begged him he should tell me the truth where he was between eight o'clock and midnight last night, and if he had any witnesses he should give their names to the police. But Mendel just shook his head and told me he wasn't any murderer but he couldn't say no more than that. And anyway what did it matter, since a no-good like him deserved only the worst?

"So when I saw I couldn't make him act sensible, I changed the subject and asked him Mama's question. 'After your fight with your Papa last night did you change your clothes before you ran out of the apartment?'

" 'When did I have time to change my clothes?' Mendel said. 'I got home, Papa and I yelled at each other, I ran out. I wore the clothes I was wearing all day long. And why please do you want to know?'

"But how could I tell him why? I didn't *know* why I wanted to know. So I kissed him across the table and told him he shouldn't lose hope, then I went away to ask the rest of Mama's questions. On account of the murder Friedman had closed the shop this morning, so I went to the building where Grossfeld lived. He had four rooms on the top floor—and his wife was lying in the bed smelling like medicine, and his kids, all five of them, were making enough noise for a hundred.

"It wasn't easy to make my voice shout above the racket. But I finally asked Grossfeld, 'Can you tell me please—before Mendel left the party yesterday, was he sick maybe from the champagne? Did he go to the men's room to be sick?'

"This was another question I couldn't make any sense out of. What did it matter if Mendel was sick or well? If a man commits a murder, they wouldn't let him go because he had an upset stomach at the time. 'As a matter of fact,' Grossfeld answered me, 'Mendel *did* get sick. It came over him just as he was getting ready to leave. He went running to the men's room and stayed there ten minutes, and when he came out he was looking a little green in the face.' I thanked Grossfeld, and then I headed for the rooming house where Sadie Katz was killed.

"The police were standing in front of it, and I had to convince them I had important business inside. Finally I got in to the Spiegel apartment, where Mrs. Spiegel was lying on the sofa, still being in a state of shock from finding a dead body, and Mr. Spiegel was fanning her head. But underneath the shock I could see in Mrs. Spiegel's eye a pleased look, from being the center of attention.

"I apologized for disturbing her at such a time—which was enough encouragement for her to tell me the whole story of her terrible experience. But finally I managed to ask Mama's question— which was even crazier than the other two. 'The two of you are lovers of the theater, I understand. Which do you prefer, the American plays or the Yiddish plays?'

"When I asked this, they looked puzzled—not half as puzzled as I was, though! They answered me that they went most of the time to the Yiddish theater. 'The American actors talk so fast,' said Mrs. Spiegel, 'you couldn't follow the story.' 'Or understand the jokes,' said Mr. Spiegel.

"So I thanked them kindly, and went back home and told Mama what answers I had got. And right away she rubbed her hands together, and said, 'Good! In fact, perfect! I also asked a question and got an answer. With all the wailing that's going on upstairs it wasn't easy to put a word in edgewise—but finally I took Mendel's Mama aside and asked her if she wouldn't tell me please—when she emptied out her son's pockets at midnight last night, did she happen to notice how many peppermints were left in the roll? And she answered me that she didn't find any peppermints in his pockets at all. So what do you think of that, baby?'

"I said to her, 'I think I'm going to start crying in two seconds, Mama. They're accusing my Mendel of killing a woman and you're worrying that he's eating too much candy!'

"But Mama didn't get annoyed or upset at me. A woman who, at the age thirteen, hid in a closet for two hours while a pogrom was going on outside don't get ruffled so easy. 'Baby, baby,' she said, 'use

161

already the brains God gave you. You know all the facts from the murder, you heard the answers to my questions—so now you should be able to prove who is the murderer.'

"That's what Mama said to me on May fourth, at eleven o'clock in the morning, forty-five years ago. And that's what I'm saying to you now."

Mom stopped talking and gazed around at all of us. On her face was that look of satisfaction which is always there at a moment like this. She knows perfectly well that we're going to admit our stupidity and beg her for an explanation.

"I don't see it," Inspector Millner said. "The case against Mendel —your husband—looks awfully strong to me."

"The case was strong," Mom said, "as long as Mendel wouldn't come up with an alibi, with a witness who saw him where he was at the time of the murder. What Mama had to do was figure out for herself where Mendel was, so the police could find his witness even without his cooperation—"

"But if there *was* such a witness," Shirley said, "why on earth didn't he say so? Surely an innocent man wouldn't *deliberately* let people think he was a murderer!"

"Wouldn't he?" Mom's voice was very quiet. "Suppose there was something which, in his opinion, was worse than being a murderer. These words filled the room for a moment. Then the Inspector said, "What could be worse?"

"It's a question of how a person was brought up," Mom said. "What was he taught to care about and have respect for and be frightened of? But I'll show you what I mean, step by step, the way Mama showed it to me.

" 'Where did Mendel go between eight o'clock and midnight?' Mama said to me. 'He went some place where people laughed at him for wearing his hat. So what does this mean to you, baby?'

"I answered her, 'It means he went to a neighborhood where there aren't any Jews. A Jewish boy is supposed to wear his hat all the time, cold or hot, inside or outside—it's part of the religion, it shows his respect for God. In a Jewish neighborhood nobody would be surprised at seeing a boy with his hat on.'

" 'This is true,' Mama said, 'but you didn't go far enough. How many times did I tell you?—half an answer is as bad as no answer at all. Even in a neighborhood without any Jews, what's so peculiar about a boy walking along the street with his hat on? It's early in May yet, it's not so hot that hats are ridiculous."

" 'You're saying, Mama, that Mendel lied about the people laughing at him?'

" 'About that he told the truth. Why make up such a story? But the minute he mentioned those people laughing, he remembered he couldn't tell the *whole* truth about them, because if he did he'd have to explain certain things he didn't want to explain. He wasn't walking on the street when these people laughed at his hat. He was *inside* —he was indoors some place where you're supposed to take off your hat. He didn't take it off, and to the other people this was funny.'

"I was a little annoyed at myself, I admit it, for not figuring this out too. So I pretended I didn't think it was important. 'Indoors or outdoors, what's the difference?' I said. 'Maybe the people laughed at Mendel in the subway. He already told us he rode in the subway last night.'

" 'If the laughing happened in the subway,' Mama said, 'why should he lie about it and say it happened on the street? And anyway, what man ever takes off his hat in the subway? So only believe me, baby—Mendel was *inside* some place last night. Now tell me please what *kind* of place?'

"I couldn't tell her. My mind wasn't working. So Mama said, 'Think, baby, think. What about the money in Mendel's pocket?'

" 'Wait a second, wait a second,' I said—and my mind was showing signs of life again. 'On the way home from the shop last night Mendel went into a candy store and bought a roll of peppermints.'

"I could see from Mama's excited look that I was on the right track. 'So, so? What about those peppermints, baby?'

" 'He paid for them with a dollar bill and put the change in his pocket. Then he got home, had a fight with his Papa, and ran out again without changing his clothes. He took a subway, stayed out for a few hours, then decided it was time to go home. But when he went back to the subway station there wasn't any money in his pockets! What happened to his change from the dollar bill? A nickel for peppermints, a nickel for one subway ride—he should have ninety cents left. Did he get his pocket picked? Foolishness. A boy like Mendel, who isn't exactly the rich-looking type, don't attract pickpockets. He *spent* this ninety cents, Mama! This place where he went indoors, where he wouldn't take off his hat—it was some kind of store where he bought something for ninety cents.'

" 'Good, good,' Mama said. 'But what kind of store is it where you're usually expected to take off your hat?'

"I couldn't say a word. All of a sudden my mind had run down again. Mama shook her head and said, 'You made such a good start with the peppermints, baby. Why don't you finish with them already? On the way home from the shop yesterday Mendel bought peppermints. But he didn't eat them, he put them in his pocket and forgot about them. And after midnight, when he was finally asleep in his bed, his Mama went through his pockets and what did she find? No peppermints. Some time in those four hours while he was out, he ate all the peppermints. So why?'

" 'He was hungry,' I said. 'Didn't he miss his dinner?'

" 'Does a growing young man make a dinner on a roll of peppermints? There's another reason for eating peppermints, no? The reason why he bought them in the first place—'

" 'To hide the champagne on his breath from his Papa,' I said. 'But Mama, this was no reason any more—because Mendel's Papa already found out about the drinking.'

" 'Naturally—that's the point I'm making,' Mama said. 'He ate those peppermints to cover up something *else* on his breath. Maybe to cover up—'

"I broke in on her because now, as clear as daylight, I saw the truth. 'To cover up something he was *eating*! Isn't that it, Mama? The store he went to in that non-Jewish neighborhood was a *restaurant*! In what other kind of place are you supposed to take off your hat? He was hungry, he went in there, he sat at a table, and ordered something which cost him ninety cents. It must have been something *awful*, Mama—because he swallowed a whole roll of peppermints to cover up the smell of it—and when he got home at midnight, he went straight to the bathroom and got sick!'

" 'Very smart thinking,' Mama said, 'but you're sure it wasn't the champagne from the party that made him get sick in the bathroom?'

" 'No, it couldn't have been,' I said. 'He already *got* sick from the champagne. Earlier in the evening just before he left the shop. So at midnight it was something else that made him sick—something he ate at that restaurant—'

" '*Mazel tov!*' Mama said, and she looked prouder of me than I ever saw her look before. 'So tell me, baby, what was this food which gave Mendel such a sickness? What was it that he felt so ashamed of he had to cover it up with peppermints, and it upset him so much it made him sick?'

" 'Mama, I don't know!' I said, and to tell you the truth I was practically in tears. 'I don't know what he ate in that restaurant, and even if I did, how is it going to get him out of jail?'

"Mama took me in her arms and patted me on the shoulder. 'Baby, it's so simple,' she said. 'If you wasn't so worried, you'd see how simple it is. A boy like Mendel, a quiet shy boy who don't stick up for himself—last night he finally stuck up for himself, he finally told his Papa he was going to live his own life. And naturally, when he ran out of the apartment he was mad—a lot madder than some other boy would be, because Mendel's been saving up this madness for twenty-one years.'

" 'I'll show Papa,' he said to himself. 'I'll do something desperate already! He'll see that I'm not under his thumb no more!' Then Mendel got off the subway and walked for a while and saw this restaurant and decided to do the positively most desperate thing he could think of. He went into the restaurant and ordered—'

" 'Pork!' I blurted out, between sobbings and gulpings.

" 'What else?' Mama said. 'Pork or ham or bacon—the forbidden food, the food that no orthodox Jewish boy who was brought up like Mendel can eat without giving God a slap in the face. He ate the *trefe* pork, and for maybe five minutes he felt like he just did a brave wonderful thing.'

165

" 'But twenty-one years don't go down the drain in one night. All of a sudden the brave feeling went away, and Mendel was hating himself, he was full of shame, he was expecting any minute that God would bring the thunder and lightning down on his head. And worst of all, he was imagining what his Papa would say if he ever found out. Whatever happened, he couldn't let his Papa find out!'

" 'So he ran out of the restaurant and he stuffed his mouth with all the peppermints so there shouldn't be any smell of pork on his breath. Then he went home—and the idea of this forbidden food in his stomach was finally too much for him, so he got sick in the bathroom. And in the morning, when the police came and accused him of killing Sadie Katz, what a terrible pickle he was in! To clear himself he had to tell them what he was doing at the time of the murder—but this is the thing he can't tell anybody. Better the whole world should think he's a murderer than his Papa should find out he ate *trefe* food.'

"When Mama finished I was relieved and happy and mad, all at the same time. 'This is why he keeps saying how guilty he is, Mama? This is why he calls himself a sinner and a transgressor and admits he broke the law? That Mendel—how could he be so crazy?'

" 'When you're twenty-one, it's easy,' Mama said. 'So we'll save him from his own craziness, baby. We'll tell our idea to the police, and they'll check up on restaurants, and it won't be long, believe me, that somebody remembers the skinny boy who wouldn't take off his hat.'

"And Mama was right, like always. The police found that restaurant by three o'clock in the afternoon and my Mendel was out of jail by four—and at five o'clock, exactly on schedule, Mendel and I got married. And we lived happy ever after—for thirty-two years."

We were silent for a moment, and then we all talked at once.

"If your husband didn't kill the girl," Shirley said, "who on earth did?"

"What was Papa's fountain pen doing on the floor of Sadie Katz's room?" I said. "And how do you explain the phone call she got on the night she was killed?"

MOM REMEMBERS

"And why," Inspector Millner said, "did you tell us that this old case reminds you of the case we're working on now? What's the comparison between your Mendel and the Ortiz boy?"

Mom chose to answer this last question first. "I'll tell you the comparison," she said, "as soon as you answer me two questions." Then she raised a finger. "One. In the last few months, since the Ortiz boy started staying out late at night, is he spending more money than usual—wearing expensive clothes maybe, or buying fancy presents for his girl friend?"

"Evidently not. Neither his sister nor his mother has seen him in any new clothes in the last four months. And his girl, Rosa Melendez, claims he doesn't even take her out to the movies as much as he used to."

"Two," Mom said. "When he was in high school, what classes did he have in learning how to put things together and take them apart?"

"Vocational training, you mean? He never had any. He always refused to take those courses at school—maybe because his father was always telling him he *should* take them."

Mom gave a nod. "Thank you. It's what I expected. Like you said—it's an open-and-shut case."

Inspector Millner got that look of misery on his face again. "You mean, you can't help the boy? You agree with us that he's guilty?"

"I was sure you'd feel that way, Mother," Shirley said. "If ever anybody's guilt was perfectly obvious—"

"Obvious?" Mom shook her head. "Like Mama told me years ago—jumping to conclusions is the best way there is to fall flat on your face. For months this Ortiz boy goes out after dinner at night and don't come back till midnight and wouldn't tell nobody where he's been—so everybody jumps to the conclusion he's doing something crooked."

Inspector Millner said, "What *other* conclusion—"

"These robbings and killings," Mom said, "which he's supposed to be doing every night—he only does them on weekdays. On weekends, on Saturday and Sunday nights, he goes out with his girl friend

167

like always. This don't seem funny to you? A gang of robbers that takes vacations on weekends—especially on Saturday nights, when more people are likely to be drunk and walking late on the streets and carrying a lot of money?

"And another funny thing—for months this boy is doing all these robberies but instead of spending *more* money than usual he's spending *less*. So what's happening to his profits? And one answer is coming to me—maybe there *aren't* any profits, maybe there *isn't* any gang of robbers."

"But Mom," I said, "that voice the boy's father heard over the phone when the boy called up his home a week ago—"

"This voice—it's the funniest thing of all. You remember what it said, this voice? 'Who's scared of the dicks? If any copper gets in my way, I'll mow him down!' An expert on gangsters I'm not, but occasionally I read the newspapers and look at the television and listen to the kids in this neighborhood talking. Tell me if I'm wrong, but it's my opinion a young tough guy nowadays wouldn't say something like 'dicks' and 'mow him down' if his life depended on it. The popular word today is 'fuzz'—no? And if you're going to shoot somebody, maybe you'll 'blast' him or 'cool' him. But 'dicks' and 'mow him down'—this is what they used to say twenty-five years ago. In fact, this is what they're always saying in those old movies with Humphrey Bogart and Edward G. Robinson."

Inspector Millner slapped his hand down on the table. "You aren't implying—"

" 'You're right, I'm implying," Mom said. "That the voice talked like one of those old mobsters? Why not, if that's what it *was*? And where are they nowadays those old movies? On television, am I right? When Mr. Ortiz talked to his son on the phone last week, what he heard in background was an old movie on the television."

"I don't see what that proves," Shirley said. "The boy and his hoodlum friends happened to be watching TV that night—"

"Look a little harder at that phone call," Mom said. "Like Mama used to tell me—half an answer is as bad as no answer at all. Why did the Ortiz boy make that call? Because he fixed his mother's television set early in the afternoon and he wanted to find out if it was still working. But who can fix a television set just by fooling around inside it with a screwdriver? Some knowledge and experience it takes. But this boy never had any classes in vocational training at his high school. So I'm asking myself where did he learn how to fix television sets? And I'm answering by putting two and two together.

"For months he's been staying out four hours every night—he never goes out like this on Saturday or Sunday nights—he's been spending not more but less money than usual during these months—the place where he goes has a television set playing—and suddenly, out of nowhere, he's got a talent for fixing television sets.

"Does this sound to you like a boy who's robbing and killing with a gang? —or does it sound like a boy who's taking a night course in how to be a television repairman so he can get a good job and marry the girl he loves?"

Looking half encouraged and half worried, Inspector Millner started shaking his head. "But if that's what he's been doing all these months—if that's what he was doing the night of the murder—why didn't he tell us? Why didn't he ever tell his parents?"

A sad little smile was on Mom's face again. "The younger generation," she said. "You think maybe it's changed after forty-five years? A Jewish boy on the East Side, a Puerto Rican boy on the West Side—but still they're two boys, with the same feelings and hurts and foolishness inside of them. For this little Ortiz boy, like for my Mendel, some things are worse than being arrested for murder. For both these boys the most important thing is, Papa shouldn't find out their secret."

"You're being illogical, Mother," Shirley said. "Your fiancé did something that his father would've disapproved of—naturally he didn't want to be found out. But this Ortiz boy, if your theory is correct, has been doing something his father *would* approve of. So why should he try to hide it?"

"You answered your own question. Because his father *would* approve of it. In fact, when he was in high school his father *told* him to do something like this. The boy positively refused but a few months ago he decided, all by himself, that his father was right. He signed up for the night course, he's been working at it hard and steady—but how could he admit this to his father, to *such* a father? How could he give his father the satisfaction of saying 'I told you so'? A boy's pride —is there anything stronger and crazier?

"And after a while, naturally, this turned into a vicious circle—the boy wouldn't say where he went at night, and this made his father call him a bum, and this made the boy even more stubborn about keeping his mouth shut. Until finally, even when the police arrested him, he couldn't back down from his pride and confess the truth. Sure it's not logical—unless you happen to be an eighteen-year-old boy."

Inspector Millner was beaming all over. "First thing tomorrow," he said, "I'll start checking all the schools for TV repairmen! That boy's mother—she's going to be so happy—"

A shadow came over Mom's face. "I wouldn't count on this," she said.

The Inspector looked up at her uncertainly. "I don't follow—"

"The boy didn't kill the cab driver," Mom said. "But just the same, his red leather jacket and his black motorcycle cap were at the scene of the crime. You saw them running away from the cab, Davie, and your eyesight I wouldn't doubt. So if the boy wasn't wearing those things, who was?"

"He was wearing them when he went out that night, Mom. His mother and father both say so."

"Absolutely. Every night, when he went out, he wore them. Because his father didn't want him to. But what about when he got to his repairman school? He couldn't show up *there* in such a crazy outfit. He had to wear a neat clean suit there, like any other serious hard-working student. So before he reached the school every night, there had to be some place where he could take off the red jacket and put on the nice suit—and when school was over for the night, he had to go back to this place and change into the jacket again, and leave the suit for the next night.

"Where could he find such a place? A hotel room? But how could he afford it? A friend's place? But who could he trust with such a secret? One person only. His sister—what's-her-name?— Inez. She's a year older than him, she has a room in a hotel down-town, she hates their father even worse than he does. The night of the murder he left his red jacket and his black cap with her, the way he's been doing for months—and after he left for his school, she put on his jacket and his cap, the way *she's* been doing for months, and she went out to rob cab drivers. With a pair of pants it's a perfect disguise for her—because the cab driver would swear to the police that he was robbed by a boy, not a girl."

"And Rafael is a small thin boy!" I said. "He wears his hair long, like all these kids nowadays. In that red jacket and that motorcycle cap—not to mention the family resemblances—it's no wonder Palazzo identified him as the killer!"

"And it's no wonder," Mom said, "you thought you saw him running away from the scene of the crime."

There was a silence. Then a soft sigh came out of Inspector Millner. "I'll have her picked up tonight," he said. "And I guess I'll call her mother—"

Another silence, and then Shirley couldn't contain herself any longer. "That's all very well, Mother," she burst out, "but what about the *old* murder, the Sadie Katz murder? Did they ever find out who killed *her*?"

Mom turned to Shirley, smiled at her a moment, then said, "Did I forget to tell you? Excuse me, my mistake. Mama found out who killed her—naturally."

"Your mother was able to explain the fountain pen?" Shirley said. "And the phone call—when Sadie Katz seemed to be talking to your fiancé and inviting him up to her room?"

"The phone call was Mama's best clue to the real murderer," Mom said. "Why did the police think it was Mendel who made that call? Why was Mendel supposed to be the man Sadie Katz invited up to her room? She had plenty of men on the string—including somebody who never came for her at the rooming house, but always made her meet him outside—so why should the police pick on Mendel?

"Well, like Mama pointed out, it all boiled down to one thing that Sadie said to that man on the phone, 'What are you afraid of? You're still a free man, aren't you? You can do what you like.' Who could Sadie have meant by these words except a single man who was about to get married? And except for Mendel there was no such man in her acquaintance.

"But Mendel had an alibi for the murder—so Sadie *wasn't* talking to him on the phone. So, like Mama told me, 'Maybe those words didn't mean what everybody thinks. After all, who heard Sadie saying those words? Mr. and Mrs. Spiegel—two old people that just came over from Germany five years ago, that never learned English so good, that prefer Yiddish plays to American plays because they can't understand what the American actors are saying. Isn't there a good chance these two people maybe didn't hear so clearly what Sadie Katz said on the phone?'

"Mama didn't have to go on. In a flash I saw what she was getting at. 'Mama, that's the answer! The Spiegels thought that Sadie Katz said, *You're still a free man, aren't you? You can do what you like.* But what she really said was, *You're Friedman, aren't you? You can do what you like.* It was Mr. Friedman, her boss, that she was talking to on the phone. She'd been having an affair with him—he's the man who never picked her up at the rooming house, who'd been meeting her outside. He called her up that night and wanted to see her. She insisted he should come to her place—and when he said he was afraid somebody might see him, she laughed and said that a big shot like him could do what he liked.

" 'So he came to the rooming house and went upstairs with her—and maybe he told her he wanted to break off their affair—and maybe she got mad and threatened to tell his wife. So he strangled her. And as for the fountain pen, Mama —well, when Mendel got home from the shop yesterday, didn't he stand on the stoop and wave at people and show them the fountain pen? And didn't Sadie Katz run up to him at that moment and throw her arms around him and kiss him? So maybe, in his surprise, he dropped the pen, and maybe Sadie picked it up—automatically, absentminded, the way people do—and that explains what it was doing in her room!'

"I stopped talking and waited for Mama to tell me what a detective genius I was. But she only shook her head.

" 'Half answers, always half answers,' she said. 'Out of *you're still a free man, aren't you?* how could you get *you're Friedman, aren't you?*

172

Where's the *still*, and where's the *a*? Even if you didn't understand English so good, you'd notice that certain sounds were left over. What Sadie really said on the phone had to be a lot closer to what the Spiegels thought they heard.'

" 'But what *was* it, Mama?'

" 'Baby,' Mama said, 'it's a well known fact that embarrassed husbands commit a lot less murders than jealous wives.'

" '*Mrs. Friedman*? She's the one—'

" 'Why not?' Mama said. 'She found out about her husband's affair and she called up Sadie Katz on the phone and demanded to see her that night. She wanted to meet Sadie uptown, but Sadie liked the idea of making this ritzy rich woman come down to her. *What are you afraid of?* Sadie said to her. *You're Stella Friedman, aren't you? You can do what you like.* And sure enough, an hour or so later, Stella Friedman did what she liked—she strangled Sadie to death!' "

Mom stopped for a breath, then went on quietly, "At the trial, incidentally, the jury found her not guilty, on the grounds of temporary insanity."

That was the end of Mom's story. I breathed a sigh of relief. What I feared hadn't happened. She had gone through all that reminiscing about the old days, about her wedding day, but she looked as cheerful as ever.

And then my heart sank. Suddenly there were tears filling Mom's eyes.

"What's the matter?" Inspector Millner cried. "Is there anything I can do?"

"I'm all right, I'm all right," Mom said. "I was only thinking—the younger generation today, the younger generation in the old days, maybe there is a difference after all. Poor Mendel—he was ready to die so he shouldn't make his father ashamed of him. And this Ortiz boy—he was ready to die so he shouldn't make his father *proud* of him."

Slowly Mom began to shake her head. "It's a funny world we're living in these days; Mama wouldn't like it much, I think. It's a good thing maybe that she never lived to see it."

Mom lowered her eyes. A moment later she took out a handker-chief and blew her nose. When she looked up, she was smiling again. "So now for dessert," she said. "In your honor, Inspector, I baked an angel food!"

Then Mom got to her feet, and like a general at the head of his victorious army she marched out to the kitchen.

MY MOTHER, THE DETECTIVE

My Mother, The Detective: The Complete "Mom" Short Stories by James Yaffe is set in 12 point Monotype Baskerville, re-cut by Stanley Morison in 1923 from the 1754 design by John Baskerville. The book is printed on 60 pound Glatfelter supple-opaque paper. The cover painting is by Carol Heyer and the design by Deborah Miller. Thomson-Shore, Inc., printed and bound the first edition consisting of approximately one thousand copies in softcover, notch-bound, and one hundred seventy-five copies sewn in Roxite-B cloth, signed and numbered by the author. All the cloth copies include a separately printed pamphlet, "The Problem of the Emperor's Mushrooms," a Paul Dawn story by James Yaffe. *My Mother, The Detective* was published in January 1997 by Crippen & Landru, Publishers, Norfolk, Virginia, USA.